DEAD IN THE MANSION

VICTORIA MATTSEN CRIME SERIES
BOOK 4

IFEANYI ESIMAI

For Chinwe...Always.
The wind beneath my wings.

ACKNOWLEDGMENTS

My heartfelt gratitude goes out to my family and friends, whose unwavering faith in me fueled this project from the very start.

I also want to extend a special thanks to a group of incredible individuals whose generous spirit has made an indelible impact on this project, and for that, I am forever grateful.

Erik S
Nneka Anaebonam
Craig Martelle
Jenn Davidson
Chinwe Anyamele
Obioha Emezie
Renee
Okechukwu Obua
Romeo Richards
Ikenna Emeghara
Charles Onunkwo
Adaeze

Everyone of you has helped shape this journey in your own unique way, and I couldn't be more thankful. Your support has not only made these books a reality but has also inspired me as I continue to tell Detective Vikki Mattsen's story.

To all the readers, thank you for inviting Detective Vikki

Mattsen into your lives. It's been a joy to share this adventure with you.

Here's to the stories yet to be told.

PROLOGUE

Jessica Reid felt like the entrée. The eyes of the man she loved were on her. She sat in a booth at Peachebees Restaurant—giddy, happy, and relieved. She wore a white and blue tie-dye summer dress with an off-shoulder design. Her long, golden hair cascaded down to her shoulders, resembling a waterfall.

The smell of well-done steak reached her nose. The culprit was a smoking platter carried by a waiter walking by. Her mouth flooded with saliva. Maybe that's what she should have ordered instead of a chicken Caesar salad.

At thirty-two, her body wasn't the calorie burner it used to be at nineteen. Now she needed another set of eyes to monitor things she shouldn't be eating.

Jessica took a sip from her glass. The liquid cooled her inside on its way down. She loved Pinot Grigio for her dinner. It never failed to smooth the way for after-dinner activities. She couldn't wait to relax after hosting a couple on their honeymoon at her home that doubled as a bed-and-breakfast.

She batted her eyes at Vince, sitting opposite her. He smiled back. His eyes said it all, slicing through all the noise

—laughter, conversation, and cutlery clanking on dinnerware. He loved her.

Their gazes locked, their eyes piercing into each other's souls. His eyes resembled the vast blue sky, and she eagerly anticipated losing herself in their depths once they returned to her house.

His manly dinner of potatoes and steak came. He didn't start eating until her Caesar salad arrived. They focused on their plates, comfortable in the silence, only loud between people not in tune with each other.

For dessert, they both got Irish coffee.

"I hardly saw the couple," Jessica said. "I thought they would be out and about. Do touristy things like hike on the Stairway to Heaven in Vernon, for that panoramic view."

Vince nodded. "Or visit Lake Mohawk in Sparta. Take a stroll on the boardwalk while enjoying their favorite ice cream."

Jessica snapped her finger and thumb repeatedly as if it would aid her memory. "Or visit the Stirling Museum at Ogdensburg to see all those glowing gems." She thought of her ten-year-old son, Rick, and her smile widened. "Rick can't get enough of the place. Did you know that parts of the movie *Zoolander*—the one with Ben Stiller—were shot in that mine?"

Smiling, he shook his head.

Jessica knew he was humoring her, and she loved him for that. Because she owned a bed-and-breakfast in St. Ives, Sussex County, she had to be ready with tourist ideas for her guests. People came from everywhere for that holiday experience that wouldn't break the bank.

The couple had rented the whole bed-and-breakfast section of her house for the weekend. But they rarely left the room.

"Why're you smiling?"

"The couple I just saw off at the train station would have saved a lot by renting a hotel room instead."

Vince took her hand, raised it to his lips, and kissed it. "Who knows? Maybe they did it for the experience."

His hot breath bathed the back of her hand, and heat coursed through her.

He raised his eyebrows. "So, they were on their honeymoon?"

Jessica beamed. "And they seemed genuinely in love." She chuckled and lowered her eyes. "Of course they should."

Vince massaged her hand. Then he said, "When will you give me an answer?"

Jessica's inside tightened. The smile on her face faded. Why did he have to go there?

"Marry me, Jessica." He choked with emotion.

She pulled her hand back and turned away. "Vince, I've told you—I'm not ready."

"That's not good enough, Jess. When will you be ready?"

She sighed. "I don't think I ever will. You know why." She grabbed her handbag from the table. "Why don't you leave well enough alone?" She opened her purse, peeled out five twenties, and tossed them on the table. "Bye."

Jessica headed for the exit. She knew people were watching but didn't care. She'd had enough. This had to end.

The blonde receptionist smiled as she approached. She glanced over Jessica's shoulder, and her smile wavered.

"Yeah, do what you do best—run away!" Vince said, following her. He had almost caught up with her. "You always think you're better than everyone. This time, I'll deal with you."

His words tore through Jessica. Her heart could've been a tomato tossed into a blender and shredded. She yanked the door open and walked into the warm evening.

Jessica wasn't sure where she parked her red BMW X5.

She had her thumb on her car's fob keyless entry and pushed it repeatedly. Her car winked—she headed for it.

Vince's ranting got louder and closer. Her skin burned as if she were on fire. She increased her pace.

Jessica got into her car and started the engine. She lowered her window, fixed her gaze on him, and laughed sarcastically. "So, this would have been my reality if I'd agreed to marry you. Thank God for little mercies. We are through!"

Vince froze. His face turned white. He shook his head from side to side. "No, no."

"Yes, we are!"

Vince's facial features hardened. He could've been sitting on the ceramic throne, trying to squeeze one out. The veins on his neck became electric cables. His lips quivered. Without warning, he lunged forward.

Jessica floored it.

He grabbed the door, but his hands slipped off. He raised his fist. "You'll pay for this—bitch!"

CHAPTER ONE

Jessica called her friend Sally to tell her she was almost home, and to bring Rick back.

She drove into her driveway at 7:30 p.m. and pushed the button to open her garage—then changed her mind. Better that she parked in the driveway so Sally would know she was home.

For the past two hours, she'd driven around St. Ives, the event at dinner going over and over in her head. Vince's image in her rearview mirror was etched on her mind.

How did a romantic dinner, on track to end with passion, crash and burn?

It was a mutually beneficial relationship. Good company. Sex on demand. Steady-flowing two-way traffic—symbiotic. Most men would kill for that type of arrangement. But not Vince. He wanted more. But she'd always been clear.

Been there, done that, and got the scars—no marriage for her.

Had she overreacted?

Was something else bothering him? *Did he overreact?* She shook her head. They were done. The words that had spewed from his mouth, she never would *unhear.* Maybe it was time to move on.

Jessica had first ended up on her sister, Brie's street. But Brie's car had not been in her driveway. She called Brie's Nail Salon. It had gone to voice mail. She'd dialed her cell. Brie answered on the third ring.

"Hi, Jess," her sister had said and laughed. "Sorry."

"I'm at your place. You're not here." Jessica's voice was accusatory, like they'd planned to meet, and Brie disappointed her. She had wanted to talk to her about Vince.

"I know that." More laughter. "I'm at Atlantic City with Joe. We should be back later tonight...or tomorrow. I have to go. Talk to you then." Brie had hung up.

Jessica's driveway security lights came on, jolting and bringing her out of her reverie. She sighed. Tomorrow she would decide about Vince.

Jessica exited the car, locked the door with the fob, and stumped into the house.

When she opened the door, a moth tried to sneak in. She ducked, shooed it away impatiently, and entered, locking the door behind her.

The foyer never failed to amaze her. The chandelier, the size of a Volkswagen Beetle, hung from the high ceiling.

Jessica placed her car key and cell phone on a half table against a wall. She walked past the double staircase and entered the living room.

Her decor was French Empire Furniture style, popular during Napoleon's era—bold red and green everywhere. She'd gotten most of the ornate tables and chairs from thrift shops and garage sales—some from discount stores and dumpsters. The saying, One man's trash is another man's treasure, was alive and well in her home.

She was a frequent visitor to flea markets, eBay online,

and Goodwill stores, hoping to one day find a Jackson Pollock or a European masterpiece worth millions for cheap.

Jessica picked up the remote control from the center table to turn the TV on. She cocked her head. A sound came from the kitchen. She admonished herself for not making sure her home was secure once she entered. Maybe her guest forgot to lock a window or door, and an intruder entered.

They'd arrived by Uber from the train station on Friday afternoon, and she'd volunteered to drop them off when they'd left on Sunday. It never hurt to be extra friendly to your guests. Word of mouth was the most effective form of advertising in the business. And repeat customers were the best.

Pulse racing, Jessica tiptoed to the kitchen, saw the source of the noise, and exhaled. The cat clawed at the door to the cabinet holding her food. She glanced at kitty's plates. Both were empty.

"My goodness. Kitty, I'm so sorry. I forgot with all the excitement."

Jessica filled the water bowl from the tap. The cat lapped at it as soon as she put it down. The food in the cabinet was new. She put her phone down and opened it. She poured kibble into the second bowl. Kitty pounced on it.

It occurred to Jessica that Rick might want a snack when he returned. She went to the fridge to see what they had. The chocolate chip cookie dough caught her eye. That would do. She set the preheat temperature in the oven, then went to the fridge for the cookie dough.

Twenty minutes later, the smell of baking filled the kitchen.

Ding-dong.

Jessica checked the time on the microwave above the cooker. It was 8:10 p.m. "Rick, I'm coming!"

She picked up the cat food and bent to put it back in the cabinet. Kitty followed.

Jessica laughed. "Still hungry? All right, just a fistful, okay?" She placed her phone down and tried to unzip the bag. Kitty jumped, trying to get to the food.

Ding-dong.

She exhaled. "All right! God." She dropped the food in the cabinet and headed to the foyer. A shadow moved on the other side of the frosted glass in the door. Smiling, she unlocked and yanked the door open. "Hi, R—"

The word froze on her lips.

A man about Vince's height and build stood in the doorway. He smiled and adjusted the collar of his crisp white button-down shirt, then smoothing out the wrinkles on his khaki pants. His face looked familiar. A previous guest, perhaps?

Jessica smiled. "I was expecting someone else. How can I help you?"

"Sorry for dropping in so late. My sister sent me to see you."

Jessica relaxed. "Ah, I thought I'd seen you before. Who's your sister again?" The moth from earlier tried to fly in. Jessica waved her hand to ward it off. The bangles on her wrist clanked. She didn't hear the name the man said. This wasn't the first time guests had sent someone to pick up something they'd forgotten. "Come in before this moth moves in."

"Oh, okay."

Jessica opened the door wider. He stepped in.

She closed it and locked it. "So, what's your—"

It happened all at once. A sound, similar to a mosquito caught in a bug zapper, was followed by excruciating pain that shot up Jessica's neck to her head. Her brain rattled like dice getting a good shake before being rolled.

Jessica's legs melted underneath her. The next second, she was on the floor, her whole body shaking.

She glanced up. In the man's hands was a syringe. The sensation of free-falling in an elevator gripped her body, her stomach lurching toward her throat, causing nausea and panic.

Something warm engulfed her thighs. Then she smelled it. Oh God, she'd peed herself. She tried to move. Her legs—arms—refused to work.

"It's okay, Jessica. I'm going to ask you a few questions." He grabbed her neck and squeezed. "Think of it as show and tell."

CHAPTER TWO

Vikki sat outside at Flame and Frost Restaurant, not far from the shores of Lake Hopatcong, on Sunday night. Angie and Susie Mellon sat, enjoying the gentle breeze and working on their dinner. Susie, a new implant from Rhode Island, was Angie's childhood friend. They'd both grown up in St. Ives.

They were casual in matching colors, as if they'd planned it—different shades of blue jeans and white or cream-colored tops.

To Vikki, the familiar earthy odor of the freshwater lake, music, and voices drifting in and out had a nostalgic feeling. It reminded her of the happy times in her childhood living with her friend Alexis and her family.

Vikki hoped to relax. But being close to a body of water brought back memories of work. They'd dealt with a dead body in St. Ives Lake only a few weeks ago. She prayed homicides would go on vacation.

Vikki raised her Hennessy and Coke. "To new friends and reunions," she said. She clicked glasses with Susie's Corona bottle and Angie's wine glass.

"To new friends and reunions," Susie said.

"To friends and reunions," said Angie.

They all drank.

Vikki lowered her glass. She picked up some fries, dunked them in ketchup, then popped them into her mouth. Her taste buds exploded. She couldn't wait to sink her teeth into the beef burger.

Angie touched Susie's hand. "Good to see you."

"Yeah," Susie said, nodding. "Since high school. We'll cut it short."

"How long will you be around for?" Angie asked, then took a bite of her grilled chicken in a bun.

"I don't know yet. But it's good to be home. My mom is ecstatic."

"That's nice," Vikki said. "Nothing beats family and maintaining an excellent relationship with them."

"So, how did you two meet?" Susie asked.

"She was snooping around at my crime scene," Vikki said. "I was going to arrest her for interfering with a criminal investigation."

Susie's eyes bulged in their sockets. "Really?"

Vikki laughed and touched Susie's shoulder. "No. I'd moved over from New York City and wasn't a known quantity then. I was investigating a case, and nobody would talk to me. Then this reporter came to ask me how the case was going. She'd ducked under the yellow police tape to come to talk to me."

Angie threw out her hand. "I was only doing my job."

"I walked her back. Anyway, we got talking, and I told her about my frustrations with witnesses. They wouldn't speak to me. So she introduced me, and they agreed to help." Vikki took a breath. "So, what made you move back? Missing the old stomping ground?"

Susie shoveled her salad around on her plate. She sighed loudly. "Running from a domestic situation."

Vikki was about to take a bite from her burger and stopped with her mouth wide open. Her ears pricked up like those of a vigilant German shepherd. She put her food down. "Are you in danger? Is anyone trying to hurt you?"

Susie raised her head. Her eyes widened. Probably because of the severe look on Vikki's face. "No, why?"

Angie laughed. "Girlfriend, you just stoked Vikki's fire. Remember she's a detective?"

Susie threw her head back and did a silent laugh. "I must be careful of the words I use around you." She glanced at her plate and pushed the food around. "It's a problem of the heart," she whispered.

"Oh no." Angie placed a hand on her chest. "Oh no, you're sick."

"No. I'm scared of commitment...so I ran."

Vikki shrugged. "Who isn't?" Her commitment issues came to mind. "We'll meet the person when they come for you."

Angie touched Vikki's hand. "I heard you have a new hot medical examiner. Has he examined you yet?"

Heat rushed to Vikki's cheeks. Her scalp itched. She hadn't been put on the spot like this in a while. What was she going to say? Her phone rang. *Thank goodness.* She picked it up from the table. Her captain's name flashed on the screen. She gave a 'wait a moment sign' with her forefinger. "Mattsen."

"Vikki, we have a situation," Levin said, his voice loud and gruff. "Where are you?"

That was a loaded question, thought Vikki. "Chief, I'm not on call. I'm in Hopatcong—girls' night out."

"I know, Vikki. The night crew is investigating a multi-car pileup on Route 80. The detective on call is at a fire scene." There was a pause. "The case I need you on...Vikki, a ten-year-old boy is involved."

CHAPTER THREE

Vikki let out an exasperated breath. The captain was pulling her heartstrings.

"Vikki, ten-year-old Rick—Richard Reid—comes home from a play date with his classmate. He rushed into the house, looking for his mom. Instead of a warm embrace, he found her dead on the floor."

The captain was still talking, but Vikki's mind had drifted to her childhood. She'd discovered her father's dead body in the bathtub. Accidental drowning, they'd called it. Her life changed forever after that. Her heart went out to the little boy.

"Mattsen, you still there?"

"I'm here, Chief. Text me the address. I'll be there in forty-five minutes."

CHAPTER FOUR

Vikki signaled left and turned her white Ford Explorer into the driveway of number twenty-eight. The headlamps of her car swept across the victim's neighbors, huddled across the street, looking in. She made a mental note. *Sometimes the doer is among the crowd, watching.*

She checked the time on her dash, ten forty-five p.m.

The house, a huge Greek revival, was imposing—four police cruisers with flashing lights parked haphazardly in front of it.

Vikki exited her car and walked past police vehicles, peering in, expecting to see the boy who'd found the body. They were both empty.

The other two cars were a red BMW X5 and a white Jeep Compass. She climbed the stairs to the porch. Six symmetrical white columns stretching to the roof stood like sentries keeping guard. Tonight, they'd failed.

"Detective Mattsen," said a uniform standing at the top of the stairs. "I didn't know you were on call." He handed Vikki the crime log.

"Hi, John."

John Acosta was a new hire. Black hair, broad shoulders, and learning one day at a time. He resembled what Jessica envisioned Gomez would have looked like at twenty-six.

Vikki smiled. "I didn't know either." She left it at that. Her job was to make her superiors smell like roses, even when they sucked. He handed her a crime scene suit, and she put it on.

Vikki walked into the foyer. "Wow," she said in a low voice. She glanced around, wondering how much a place like this cost. Her attention went to the chandelier. If that came crashing down on someone, that would become another homicide.

The smell of baked cookie dough reminded her of the food she'd abandoned to be here. She pushed the thought away. Antique furniture was everywhere. Was robbery a motive?

"Nice decor, right?" said a deep, familiar voice.

Vikki whirled. Dennis Mallory, head of CSU for SIPD, stood in protective clothing at one entrance of a double staircase. He was that meticulous with crime scenes, too.

"Hi, Denny. They dragged you out, too?"

"We're stretched. There is a ten-vehicle pileup on 80. I came in to help."

Vikki nodded. "Duty calls."

"Protect and serve," Mallory said. "I'll go see what it looks like upstairs. I'll let you know what I find."

She watched him disappear up the stairs, then glanced around for the victim.

A female CSU tech with a bootie over high heels walked past Vikki.

"Excuse me, where's the victim?"

She pointed. "DRT." And moved on.

"Dead right there," Vikki said under her breath. Someone must be pissed off—probably dragged out of a party.

Vikki walked over to the victim. Blonde, her tie-dyed tee shirt, rode up to her thighs. *Rape?* The ME would determine that with a rape kit.

She inspected the floor around the victim. Murderers always make mistakes. There was no sign of a scuffle. Vikki hoped the ME would materialize.

There was blood around the victim's head. Her hair looked like a bunch of feathers dipped in Jell-O. She must have gone through hell.

"Mattsen! You finally made it."

CHAPTER FIVE

Vikki placed a hand on her chest and rolled her eyes. "Hi, Mike. Don't you think it's too late in the day to be raising your voice?"

"They dragged you out of a girl's night out?"

Vikki hoped he couldn't smell Hennessy on her breath. "Yeah, something like that." He looked bulky, and Vikki guessed he had his customary black suit and a white shirt, but no tie underneath his protective clothing. "I see you're already dressed for work. Waiting for the clock to strike seven in the morning."

Gomez laughed. "Good one, Mattsen. I have no life, right?" He stopped laughing like a kitchen faucet turned off. "The vic is Jessica Reid, thirty-two. The cause of death is yet to be determined. But possibly trauma to the head. We'll wait for the medical examiner, ME, to give us the exact cause. It seems like she knew the perp."

Vikki cocked her head. "Why do you think so?"

Gomez got on his haunches and pointed at Jessica's wrist. "Her wrist is at an odd angle. Defensive wound? There doesn't seem to be much struggle, though."

"Maybe," Vikki said, "she was baking. Maybe it wasn't the person she was expecting."

Gomez's knee popped as he got up. "She was expecting her son. His aunt drove him back. He found the body."

Vikki pursed her lips and glanced around. "I like her furniture style."

Gomez contracted and extended his right knee, wincing. "She ran a B & B and was also an interior decorator. Self-employed."

Vikki scanned her surroundings. "Where's the son?"

She noticed a boy sitting on a chaise lounge beside a red-haired woman. His ears stuck out like Will Smith's. The woman next to him was in shock. Against her pale skin, her hair appeared like it was on fire.

"Oh Jesus," Vikki muttered. "You left them here?"

"Of course not," said Gomez, lowering his voice. He spoke through clenched teeth. "I told Acosta to put them in a cruiser or take them to the station."

"He probably forgot. He's in front with the crime log." She walked over to them.

The woman raised her head. Her eyes were red. She pulled the sobbing boy closer to her in a tight hug.

"I'm Detective Victoria Mattsen," Vikki said softly. "I'm so sorry for your loss. Are you his aunt? What are your names?"

"I'm Sally Bolton... He's Richard Reid...Rick." She shook her head. "Jess...Jessica and I are friends. He calls me aunt."

"Oh, I see. I want to ask you a few questions, if you don't mind?"

"Someone already did. I want to get him out of here."

The boy glanced from Vikki to Sally, then he sobbed. His shoulders shook. The woman brought him closer to her.

"I agree with you," Vikki said. "But we must gather information while it's fresh in your mind. It would—"

"I-I just want to go home and see if Rick can get some sleep," Sally said, wiping her eyes with the back of her hand.

Two shafts of headlights beamed in through the glass window.

Vikki looked out. The familiar shadow of the coroner's truck was unmistakable. She thought fast. Getting information while it was still fresh was very important. But the woman and child shouldn't see the ME at work.

"Okay, I'll have an officer drive you to the station. I'll take your statement—then you're free to go."

Sally did a soft head shake. "That sounds good."

Vikki led the way, and Sally and Rick followed.

Outside on the porch, Vikki said to Acosta, "Please take Ms. Bolton and Rick to the PD. Please make sure they're comfortable in interview rooms one or two. I'll be right there."

Acosta opened his mouth to say something, changed his mind, and closed it. "Will do, ma'am."

Vikki leaned closer and said in a low voice, "Please don't call me ma'am. I'm not your mother."

"Yes, sir."

Vikki would have laughed if the circumstances were different. She kept a straight face and directed them to Acosta's cruiser.

Dr. Brandon strolled past with two assistants laden with equipment. "Detective Mattsen."

Vikki smiled and nodded. She exhaled and shifted her gaze outside through the window. She hoped none of the looky-loos would be bold enough to cross the yellow tape with Acosta gone. But they still needed to get information from them.

Back inside, Jessica bumped into Detective Santiago. "Hi, I didn't know you were here."

"Captain Levin asked me to come and help."

Vikki instructed her to get information from the onlookers. "Whoever is willing to talk. Ask about home security cameras. Get their contact information, too."

Dr. Brandon had everything in place as Vikki reentered the living room. He took many photos, two from every angle. The mechanical double shutter sound of his Canon camera filled the living room.

Two CS investigators were close by, gathering fingerprints and fibers from around the victim.

Vikki watched Brandon snap on gloves, pick up a scalpel, and raise the victim's dress to her chest. She looked away while he took the body's temperature.

"Detective Mattsen," said a familiar voice.

Vikki turned, happy for the distraction. Mallory stood at the base of the stairs.

The CSU's chief's eyes twinkled with excitement. "Detective—there's a wall safe upstairs, and it's wide open."

CHAPTER SIX

"Robbery was the motive for this?" Vikki said as she and Gomez walked up the stairs behind Mallory. She hoped they would find clues that would point them somewhere.

"We'll see," Gomez said.

At the top of the stairs, Mallory made a right. Vikki followed, but glanced behind her. The corridor ended in a wall with a door. She remembered the double staircase downstairs. Did they lead to different sections of the house? She stopped and jerked her thumb toward the wall with the door. "The corridor is not continuous?"

"I think she used that part of the house as a bed-and-breakfast," Mallory said.

"There are four self-contained rooms in that part of the house," Gomez said. "One was occupied recently or hasn't been readied for the next guest."

Vikki sighed. She prayed many guests hadn't passed through the house. Otherwise, it would be a cesspool of DNA like a hotel room. But it gave them a place to start their investigation. She must have a list of her guests somewhere.

"Have the investigators gotten there yet?" Vikki asked.

"Not yet, but we will," Mallory said and continued walking.

The decor upstairs was the same taste as downstairs, but subtle. They passed two rooms with open doors and investigators inside. One was a young boy's room with a poster of Pokémon on the wall. Vikki knew that being into Pokémon was a rite of passage for kids his age in the States.

Jessica's son's gaming chair butted against a table with a curved computer screen.

The other room they passed looked like a hotel suite, probably used as a spare room.

Mallory led them into an enormous bedroom. It was the victim's room. A picture of her and her son hung on the wall. Another picture frame was on her table.

Several dresses lay on the four-poster bed with ornate carvings on the headboard. She must have tried on a few before deciding on the one.

"Her home office is in there," Mallory said, pointing at an open door inside the room.

Vikki noticed an executive table, complete with a sizable monitor. They'd need a warrant to get to her PC.

On the wall was a famous framed painting of Napoleon sitting on a rearing horse on a snow-covered mountainside, his bright-red cape whipped by the wind. Someone had already pulled back the picture frame like a door. The door to the safe was open too.

Mallory gestured with his hand. "It's a combination safe— measures about thirteen inches wide, twenty inches high, and eight inches deep. There's no evidence of tampering. As you can see, it's empty. And wiped clean of fingerprints." He leaned forward and sniffed. "I can smell what used to be there. It's made of highly absorbent material and holds the odor of anything it comes in contact with. From the inks and metal of the printing press to anywhere it was stored."

Vikki was thinking of bonds or certificates. Wasn't that old school? "Who takes possession of such things?"

Gomez came closer to the safe entrance and sniffed. "Money?"

Mallory gushed like a child. "Yes." Then he composed himself. "I would guess there were other things stored in here. It's a typical combination safe. I think they persuaded her to open it."

Vikki shook her head. In her years on the force, she'd seen a lot. People had killed for less. If robbery was the motive, how much was in there? What else had Jessica Reid had in the darned safe?

CHAPTER SEVEN

Vikki walked down the stairs.

Investigators with their gear went up the other staircase toward the section used as a bed-and-breakfast. The ME was ready at the bottom of the stairs, the victim in a body bag about to be wheeled out.

Brandon smiled. "We're all set. I'm sure you'd like to know the time of death."

"Yes, please."

He locked eyes with her for a second longer, then glanced at the body bag. "When we arrived, the victim's body was still warm. Based on temperature and lividity, I would place the time of death about three to four hours ago. And that should be between eight and nine p.m. She has what seems to be a blunt trauma on her left temple and a left arm fracture."

Vikki's eyes were on him, expecting more. His nostrils flared. If he were white, he would have blanched. She realized she'd been staring and looked away.

"I-I have no more information until I get her to the lab," Brandon said.

Vikki gave a subtle nod. "Thanks."

Their eyes met again. She lowered her gaze. *Lady, get a grip on yourself. You are at a crime scene.*

Dr. Brandon must have given a sign to his technicians because the gurney rolled away.

Vikki turned around, saw Mallory talking to Gomez, and strolled over. He painted a picture of what he thought had happened—how the crime had gone down.

"I think the bell rang," Mallory said. "She answered the door, and the person was not a threat to her."

"Someone she knew?" Vikki asked.

Mallory cocked his head. "Maybe, or she was being polite."

To her detriment, Vikki thought.

"She invited the person in," Mallory said. "At some point, the person must have persuaded her...with intimidation. A gun or knife to take her upstairs and open the safe."

Adrenaline surged through Vikki. "That means the perp must have known that what they sought was in the safe."

Mallory led the way to the stairs. "It's possible. Up the stairs, they went."

Vikki and Gomez followed. They headed to the open safe.

Gomez cocked his head. "What happened next?"

"She opened the safe. The perp emptied the contents into a bag, probably. Then they went down."

"She cooperated," Gomez said. "Why kill her?"

Mallory drew in a deep breath and exhaled. "Either that was the intention all along, or something went wrong, and the person had to change their plan and leave in a hurry." Mallory shrugged. "That's my theory for now. As we analyze the evidence we've gathered, it might change."

"Shall we go through the other section together?" Vikki asked.

"We could," Mallory said with a sigh. "But my men have

collected what they could from the scene. And I've done a walk-through myself. Only one room was used."

Vikki trusted Mallory's judgment. He was once a homicide detective and understood the process.

"I read about a similar case years ago," he said. "I think it was in New Hampshire. The guests of a bed-and-breakfast would steal from their host on their way out." Mallory squeezed Vikki's shoulder. "Anyway, feel free to look at that section. We're done with the scene. I'll see you guys in a few hours." He walked toward the door.

Gomez glanced at his watch. "It's way past midnight. You want to check it out?"

The mention of time reminded Vikki that she was supposed to be somewhere else. "Oh shit." She smacked her forehead with her palm. "The son and Sally are waiting at the PD."

"I've already seen the place myself," Gomez said. "And we can always come back. I tried to talk to the boy earlier, but he was too distraught. I can't even imagine how he feels."

But I can, thought Vikki. She'd been there twice. It was scary and uncertain.

"Let's go talk to Sally Bolton."

CHAPTER EIGHT

Vikki and Gomez drove to the PD. By then, it was almost one a.m.

The office always felt different at night. Maybe because the detectives and uniforms working at night differed from the usual ones, she saw during the day.

Vikki grabbed two cups of coffee from the break room, then went to the interview room. The liquid mud was the one thing that was consistent on night or day shifts.

She peered through the one-way window into interview room one. Rick and Sally were there. Rick's head rested on his folded hands. His hair was black compared to his mother's blonde. Maybe he took after his father.

His big ears stuck out. The type of ears other kids at school would make fun of. Saliva dribbled from the corner of his slightly open mouth onto the back of his hand. He was fast asleep.

Emotion tugged at her heart. So many years ago, she, as a little girl, had been in a police station interview room after her stepfather and mother died on the same day.

Vikki's gaze shifted to Sally, and she jerked back. She sat

next to Rick. Her wide, red eyes seemed to stare straight into hers.

Vikki had been on the other side countless times and knew you could not see the outside. But, Jesus, it looked like Sally could.

Gomez walked up. "Ah, you brought coffee." He reached for one.

Vikki moved her shoulder to shield the drink. "You can get yours when you go to get a Coke."

Gomez frowned. "Get a Coke."

"Yes, when you take the boy out, when I interview Sally."

Gomez shook his head, knocked once, and opened the door. "Hello, Sally, Rick."

Vikki passed one cup to Sally.

Sally's eyes showed how tired and worried she was. She took the cup and said, "Thank you."

"Sorry, it took us a bit of time to get here. We had to ensure we did a thorough job of gathering evidence and securing the building." She pulled out one chair opposite Sally and Rick.

Rick stirred, opened his eyes, and closed them. He sat up with a start. He wiped his mouth with the back of his hand. "Hello."

"Hi, Rick," Vikki said. "Taking a nap?"

Rick nodded, then said, "Did you find Kitty? My Aunt Brie won't be happy if I lose her."

"Not yet," Gomez said. "But we'll find her. Where's your aunt?"

"At her home here in St. Ives," Rick said.

"Can we go home now?" Sally asked.

Vikki gave an apologetic shrug. It was more complicated than that. One thing after the other. "It's only going to take a few minutes. Unless you want to come back in the next four hours." That was a lie, but sometimes you had to bend the truth.

Sally sighed. "Okay."

Gomez smiled at the boy. "Rick or Richard. Which one do you go by?"

"His mother...calls him Rick," Sally said. The last three words faded to nothingness.

"All right, Rick, come with me. Let's get you something to drink, and you can tell me all about Kitty." Gomez reached for the door.

Sally blinked rapidly. Her gaze darted from Vikki to Gomez. "Where are you taking him?"

"It's okay, Sally," Vikki said. "They'll be right back. Just to the break room."

Rick didn't move. He turned to Sally.

"I'll be right here," Sally said with a slight nod.

Gomez waved him forward, not waiting for an answer.

Rick got up and followed him.

Once they'd shut the door, Vikki said, "I'm so sorry for your loss. This won't be easy on you. I'll be asking you questions about his mother. It would've been hard on him."

Sally lowered her eyes and touched her neck. "I understand."

Vikki glanced at the video camera at a corner in the ceiling. The light was on. The entire session would be recorded. She brought out a notepad. "So what happened when you got to the house?"

Sally inhaled and blew out a breath. "Rick and Tony had a play date."

"Who's Tony?"

"My son—he and Rick are classmates."

Vikki scribbled 'Tony' on her notebook. Her forehead furrowed. "So where is he?"

"He's at home with his father."

"What's his father's name?"

Sally hesitated. "Am I a suspect? Do I need a lawyer?"

"You're not a suspect. We're only gathering information to make sense of what happened."

"My husband's name is Will, William Bolton."

Vikki nodded. "What do you do for a living?"

"I'm a nurse at the psychiatry hospital in Denville."

Vikki wrote in her notebook. "So, what happened?"

"So, Jessica calls and says her date ended early. She was home, so I could bring Rick back earlier than planned. So when I brought him back...as soon as I stopped, he was out of the car. He ran toward the house, up the stairs." Tears flowed down Sally's face, but her voice was steady.

"What time was that?"

"I'm not sure, maybe about nine p.m. Tony stayed back because tomorrow is school. I'd planned to talk with Jess and find out about her date." Her voice cracked. "Then I heard Rick scream. I ran into the house...and saw. I froze. She lay there, blood around her head. Then I realized the pain in my hand was from squeezing my phone so tight. I called nine-one-one."

The interview lasted about an hour. Jessica and Sally had met because of their boys. They wanted playdates after school, and the mothers had to make it happen. The other thing they had in common was that they were both divorced and age mates. Sally was thirty.

"Do you know anyone who might want to hurt her?" Vikki asked.

Sally shook her head. "'Everyone liked her."

"Was she butting heads with anyone?"

"Not to my knowledge."

"I almost forgot," Vikki said. "What's her date's name?"

"Vince. Vince...Vince Ramsey. I think he works at a publishing company."

Vikki wrote the name on her notebook and slapped the pen down on it. "Okay, that's good."

Moments later, Gomez stepped into the room with Rick. He had a can of Coke in his hand.

"Can I take Rick home now?" Sally said.

Vikki knew that would not happen. Rick was ten years old. He would only be released to a family member or stay temporarily with the police. "Do you have Jessica's sister's number?"

CHAPTER NINE

Vikki returned to her three-bedroom apartment on the second floor around three a.m. It was an open-floor layout. She had a couch, a coffee table, and a flat-screen TV she rarely watched. A circular dining table with three chairs adorned the dining/kitchen area. Vikki Mainly used it for files and folders when she brought work back. The only thing that was used regularly was her coffee maker.

Wouldn't it be great if Dr. Brandon was waiting for her when she returned home instead of an empty apartment? Maybe she should get a cat. She already had some of the same psychopathic traits cats have—boldness, pet-unfriendliness, human-unfriendliness, and meanness.

In her bedroom, Vikki put her gun away in the biometric safe under her bed. She went to the bathroom, turned on the shower to let the cold water warm, and removed her clothes. Her thoughts drifted to the last hour at the PD. Had she been mean to Sally?

She'd tried Jessica's sister's number, but her phone was off. Sally Bolton had been almost hysterical when Vikki had informed her that Rick would not be going home with her.

Sally had argued and pleaded. "His mother trusted me on a play date with my son."

But circumstances had changed, and sometimes weird things happened. Vikki hadn't said that to her. She'd only said, "There are guidelines we must follow regarding minors."

Sally had stayed with Rick until arrangements were made with the state Department of Children and Family Services (DCFS), and a Child Protective Services (CPS) worker was assigned to him. Vikki was a living example of what might go wrong when there were no attempts to get things done right.

Vikki was toweling herself dry when her phone rang. She answered.

"Angie, why are you calling this late?" The cop in her took over, remembering Susie said she was running from something. "Is your friend Susie *really* okay?"

"Glad I got you," Angie said. "Calm down, Vikki. Susie is fine. Remember, she was running from matters of the heart, not from a serial killer."

"So, why are you calling?"

"I need information. You drove away from Lake Hopatcong like you had a bug up your ass."

Vikki sighed. Angie's job as a crime reporter for the *St. Ives Chronicle* could sometimes be demanding.

"Any insider scoop about the murder? Apart from the fact that she lives in a million-dollar home. She is a single mother and was discovered by her son, bludgeoned to death. What's the motive?"

"That's way too much information. We don't even have an official cause of death yet. Who told you all that?"

"Don't worry about that. At least you know it wasn't you. Let's say someone close to SIPD." Angie sighed. "Vikki, I'm trying to help you. I need confirmation. We're running a story tomorrow morning about the murder—you're the dick in charge, right?"

"I'm the...detective in charge."

Angie let out a happy giggle. "I'm so happy I caught this. The headline I came up with is on point—MURDER IN THE MANSION. I called my sources after you left. Anyway, at the end of my report, I can say: If you have any information at all, please get in touch with Detective Victoria Mattsen at one, two, three, blah blah blah. That's it. Try to get some sleep."

"Goodnight, too." Vikki hung up.

CHAPTER TEN

Vikki walked past Jody's desk at 9:05 a.m. the next day.

"Hi, Vikki," Jody said.

"Good morning," Vikki said, yawning.

"Somebody didn't get enough sleep last night."

"You can say that again." Vikki continued toward the detective squad room.

Jody stifled a yawn.

Vikki had barely shut her eyes last night after speaking with Angie when it was time to get up again. She was glad to be out of her jeans and into something more formal—a beige pantsuit.

She'd stopped to get coffee from Dunkin, and the few sips she'd taken were the only reason she could function now. Vikki entered the office, and Gomez was already sitting at his desk. He gave her a nod.

In the background, someone complained that he should be informed before people working under him were assigned duties in the middle of the night. Vikki smiled. Detective McClane was always complaining.

Gomez raised his hand and waved. "Hey, McClane! You

know you can take that up with the chief. In case you're wondering, he's in the office now."

"Shut up, Gomez!"

Vikki handed Gomez a cup of coffee. She didn't get a Box O' Joe this time.

"Thank you," Gomez said with emphasis on 'you.' "I stared at the ceiling the rest of the night. This will be my first excellent coffee in the morning. I hope it does the trick."

Vikki approached her desk. The light on her intercom was blinking. She had a message.

Gomez lifted his hands, palms facing outward, signaling a 'hold it right there' stance. "Don't sit. Don't sit. Levin wants us to brief him as soon as you come in." He headed for the captain's door.

Vikki blew out a breath and followed. "This is now a relay race where we hand the baton over to ourselves from one shift to another."

The phone on Vikki's desk rang. She looked over her shoulder.

"You'll get it later," Gomez said and knocked on the captain's door. "Let's see what the chief has to say." He grinned. "I guess the mayor wants us to sort this out as soon as possible."

Vikki thought about Rick. He had classmates. They had parents and grandparents. Angie's news piece in *St. Ives Examiner* would've been delivered to their homes already. People would worry.

"Vikki, thanks so much for rising to the occasion," Captain Levin said in his deep, gruff voice. "I owe you one."

"What about me?" Gomez said, smiling.

"You've already been rewarded by letting her lead."

Gomez protested, "She's my pupil."

"But somewhere along the way, the pupil overtook the teacher. Mattsen has long passed that point." Levin waved his hand as if to unscramble what was being said and start afresh. "Where are we with yesterday's murder?" He pointed at the chairs across from him.

Vikki looked at Gomez. He gave a slight nod.

Vikki sat and said, "The victim was thirty-two-year-old Jessica Reid. She was an interior decorator and ran a bed-and-breakfast from her home."

"She lived there, too?"

Vikki nodded. "Cause of death was blunt force trauma to the head, awaiting the ME's confirmation. No murder weapon has been recovered yet. We think maybe the victim knew the perp. Motive...we're looking at robbery for now. A wall safe in her room was empty, and the door ajar."

Levin clasped his hands. When he spoke, his voice was solemn. "The mother's friend wanted to take the son home with her."

Vikki sighed. She still wasn't sure if she had done the right thing. "Ms. Bolton was adamant, but..."

"You did the right thing," Levin said. "It was an emergency. The mother was dead. The father is not in the picture. DCFS will try to place the child with relatives. Any relatives close by?"

"Yes, there's a sister," Gomez said. "Mattsen tried to reach her last night, but her phone was off. We'll follow up this morning."

There was a knock, and the door opened. Jody, the department's admin, barged in. Only she had earned the right to do that. She waved a pink slip in her hand, her gaze glued to Vikki's face.

"I thought you were at your desk. I've been calling you." She was flushed.

"No, I came straight to the—"

"Here." Jody cut her off. "This girl, Sandra, has been calling since you got in. She said she saw the headline in St.

Ives Examiner about the murder and thinks the victim was at their restaurant yesterday evening. Call her! Or go see her." Jody shook her head and walked off.

Vikki stared at the paper, her heart doing flips. That was precisely what they were looking for. The message read: Sandra Rollo. Peachebees Restaurant on Franklin Street. So it was good speaking with Angie early this morning.

CHAPTER ELEVEN

Vikki signed out a car. She drove to Peachebees Restaurant with Gomez riding shotgun.

Once they entered the reception area, the receptionist saw them and stiffened.

Vikki glanced at her name tag and smiled. "Sandra Rollo?"

The girl nodded. Her shoulder-length blonde hair bobbed up and down. Her nostrils flared. She looked like a ghost inside her black shirt and black pants uniform.

"Are...are you the police?"

"Yes, I'm Detective Victoria Mattsen." Vikki unclipped her badge from her belt and held it up. "My partner, Detective Mike Gomez. Sorry I missed your call. We came as soon as I got your message."

"Is there a place we can talk in private?" Gomez asked, putting away his badge.

"I'll-I'll let the manager know. I'll take my fifteen-minute break now." Sandra left them at the reception area and walked toward the bar.

"She's scared," Gomez said.

"Of course. When you were her age, how many people did

you come in contact with one day, only to learn they'd been murdered the next?"

"You're right. It doesn't matter the person's age. Anyone would have been rattled."

A few seconds later, Sandra returned with a man, probably in his late twenties.

"Hi, I'm Jason, the manager." He shook hands with Vikki and Gomez. "You can use my office. It's a good thing the breakfast rush is over."

Vikki felt the young man was too eager to hand over his office. He might 'forget' his cell phone and record their conversation. "Don't worry. I need some fresh air. We'll sit at the table outside."

Once outside, Sandra said, "Mind if I smoke?"

Vikki would have preferred she didn't, but they were outside, and you didn't look a gift horse in the mouth. She brought out a pen and her notebook. "Not at all."

Sandra took a pack of Camels from her pocket, her hands shaking. She extracted one, placed it on her lips, and had a harder time using her lighter. She took a deep drag once it lit and blew out wavy smoke.

"Start from the beginning, after they came in," Vikki said.

"The lady asked for a booth for two. I picked up the menu and led them to an available table. It was a busy evening, and I attended to other customers." Sandra raised her cigarette to her lips with shaky hands. "The second time I noticed them was after about forty-five minutes."

Vikki knew it wasn't in the best interests of the interview to interrupt someone volunteering information, but her curiosity was piqued. "what drew you to them?"

A silly grin appeared on Sandra's face. "He was a dead ringer for Ben Simmons of the Brooklyn Nets."

"The basketball player?" Gomez asked.

A flush of red appeared on Sandra's cheeks and neck. She

turned away and took another drag of her cigarette. This time, she blew out the smoke in a straight line.

Vikki tried not to smile. The girl had a crush. "Please go on."

"The woman stomped out, looking pissed. The man was behind her, trying to catch up. He said something like, 'Do what you do best—run away. You think you're better than everyone. This time I'll deal with you.'"

Gomez raised an eyebrow. "He said he'd deal with her?"

Sandra took another drag, then crushed her cigarette in an ashtray.

Vikki heard voices behind them and turned. Two couples, smiling and talking, headed for the door. The manager glanced through the restaurant's window at them now and then.

"What happened next?" Vikki asked.

"They continued to the parking lot. It was obvious the woman was about to leave. She headed to a red Bimmer."

Vikki raised an eyebrow. "BMW?"

Sandra nodded. "The woman got in the car. They were still talking, but out of range to hear. Then she drove off."

Vikki glanced at the restaurant again. The manager guided newcomers to their seats. Sandra's back was to the restaurant. They would need her soon.

"How did you hear about her?" asked Gomez

"I thought little about it until I arrived at work. We still get the local paper delivered. I'd picked it up by the front door when I saw the image of the woman. Your phone number was on the story, so I called."

The manager walked toward them.

Vikki brought out her business card. "Call me if you remember anything more, and thanks so much for being a good citizen."

CHAPTER TWELVE

After hearing from Sandra Rollo, Vikki asked for uniforms to pick up Vince Ramsey.

"If he asks why, tell him it's about an altercation last night at Peachebees Restaurant. We need to hear his side of the story."

Vince Ramsey owned Ramsey Publishers—a small publishing company that created custom print books for independent publishers and sometimes the big five.

Vikki watched from the one-way mirror while waiting for Gomez. Vince Ramsey sat in interview room one, hands on the table, twiddling his thumbs. His sky-blue, button-down shirt, gray vest, and pants seemed tailored. He picked up his cell phone, tapped on the screen, brought the phone to his ear, then frowned at the phone.

Vikki walked into the room with Gomez behind her.

Mr. Ramsey looked up and said, "About time. Did Jessica put you up to this? I don't know why I allowed those officers to talk me into coming here with them."

"Mr. Ramsey, I'm Detective Victoria Mattsen. My partner, Detective Mike Gomez. Sorry for keeping you waiting."

Gomez gave him an apologetic smile. "We got into a little traffic jam on our way here. Can I get you something to drink? Water? Coke?"

Mr. Ramsey raised his hands. "No, I'm fine. We're all here now. Let's get this over and done with."

"We're going to record this session so that we can get it... over and done with," Gomez said, enunciating the last four words. He pointed at the green light in the ceiling. "Is that okay?"

They didn't need his consent to record. Vikki knew Gomez was angling to give a semblance of good faith.

Mr. Ramsey jerked his head in that direction. He hesitated. "Okay." He swung back to face them. There was a tightness in his eyes. "Jessica put you up to this, right? Where is she? I've been trying her number. It goes straight to voice mail."

Vikki shook her head. He didn't know? Or was ignorance part of his defense? "No, a concerned citizen saw the altercation in the parking lot."

"Yeah, right," Mr. Ramsey said and laughed. "The US of A. Once they see a black man arguing with his girlfriend, who happens to be white, it becomes an altercation." He flapped a hand in dismissal. "Give me a break."

Gomez shrugged. "So, what happened?"

Mr. Ramsey leaned forward. "Nothing happened. We met for dinner, ate, and had an argument like any other normal couple, period."

"An eyewitness said you threatened her," said Vikki.

Mr. Ramsey inhaled and blew air out of his lips as if deflated. "Okay, we've been going out for about two years, and I thought it was time we moved our relationship to the next level."

Gomez raised an eyebrow. "Which is?"

"Marriage, of course." Mr. Ramsey gave Gomez a look

that suggested he wasn't as bright as he appeared. "She had dropped off a couple at the train station and told me they'd spent their honeymoon holed up in their room at her bed-and-breakfast. She uses a section of her home as a bed-and-breakfast."

Mr. Ramsey dropped his head. He focused on his hands. When he continued, his voice was low and sad.

"I asked her to marry me...and she overreacted. I, too, overreacted. She got up and left. I followed her to the parking lot and said things I shouldn't have said." He sighed. "I've been calling her to apologize, but she's not answering. I guess she's still mad at me."

Vikki was impressed. *Either he's an excellent actor, or he doesn't know what happened last night.*

"You must have been angry, too," Gomez said.

Mr. Ramsey nodded. "I was."

"So, you followed her to her house. Emptied her safe and hit her head with a blunt instrument."

Mr. Ramsey's head shot up. He snorted laughter, eyes on Gomez. "You've lost your mind. You guys must be rent-a-cop or something." His eyes darted from Gomez to Vikki. "Why would I hit her? I love her."

Gomez continued. "You struck her so hard you cracked her skull. Jessica is dead."

The smile on Mr. Ramsey's face vanished. He sprang to his feet. "What? Jessica, dead?"

CHAPTER THIRTEEN

"Please sit down, Mr. Ramsey!" Gomez said.

The look on Vince Ramsey's face was total disbelief.

Vikki watched, somewhat surprised by his reaction. He wobbled, then collapsed onto his seat.

"Oh my God... Oh my God." Mr. Ramsey clasped his head between his palms and pulled at his hair.

Vikki felt sorry for him. Whether or not he was responsible, someone he cared for was dead. She gave him a few moments to grieve before continuing with the questioning.

"I'm sorry for your loss, but where were you between eight and nine p.m. yesterday?"

Mr. Ramsey looked up. Tears trickled down his face. "I can't believe this. Do you still think I would hurt Jess? I've already told you everything I know. Am I a suspect?"

Vikki shook her head. "Right now, we can say you're a person of interest. The bottom line is that we're investigating a crime. Help us establish where you were when this crime was committed."

Vince Ramsey seemed to contemplate what to say. His lips moved. He exhaled, the breath rattling out of him.

Vikki felt he was hiding something. Did he want to confess? That would be great for everybody. She glanced at the ceiling to make sure the camera was still on. The green light was still lit. She resisted filling the silence.

"Maybe I should call Gerry now," Vince Ramsey said.

"Whose Gerry?" Gomez asked.

"My lawyer."

Vikki's stomach tightened. Once he called in 'Gerry,' he would advise him not to say a word. Vikki wanted to say something but didn't want to appear too pushy. But Gomez didn't care.

"Listen, Vince. Tell us exactly what happened. Sometimes things get out of hand. If it comes from you, we work with and know the DA. He will have a sympathetic ear. But, if we investigate and reach the same conclusion, you'll get the full penalty."

Vince Ramsey looked like a drowned rat. Vikki expected him to cave any minute.

"After Jess drove away, I was dazed. I got in my car and drove to Amara, my secretary's house. She was getting in her car, about to run some errands. Then she would watch a movie. I went with her. You can ask her."

Gomez snorted. "Your secretary? Very convenient."

Vince Ramsey fixed his gaze on Gomez. "I had to buy a ticket. You can confirm with AMC."

"Which movie did you watch?" Vikki asked.

He told her.

They asked him the same questions in different ways for the next forty-five minutes, trying to see if he would change his story, but he was consistent.

Gomez said he'd be right back and left the interview room.

Vikki sighed. They were back to square one.

"What about Rick?" Mr. Ramsey asked. He shook his head. "Poor boy—where's he?"

"He's with Child Protective Services. It was—"

"What? Her sister refused to take him? I didn't know Brie hated her sister, too. I thought it was only me she despised. She was always bad-mouthing me. I believe she did this to get back at me."

Vikki raised an eyebrow. "Murder her sister to get back at you?"

"Not get back at me. To stop me from becoming a spouse and the privileges that come with it. She's the one who had been poisoning Jessica's mind. She believes that somehow, I'm after Jessica's money."

There was a pause. "Are you?"

"No. I have my own money and own my business."

There was a knock on the door. Gomez stepped in. He whispered in Vikki's ear, "His alibi checked out. We must let him go."

Vikki wasn't surprised. She'd expected it. But this sister angle she hadn't considered. Was she getting slack? Vikki assured herself she would have gotten to it in due course.

"Thank you for your time," Gomez said. "I'll arrange a car to drop you back at your office. I hope you don't have any vacations planned. Don't leave town without letting us know."

Vikki held up her card. "Thank you for coming in. Please call if you remember anything else."

Vince Ramsey stood, and so did Vikki. He seemed to have regained some composure. Channeling anger toward Jessica's sister must have done the trick. But this was only the beginning. People grieve differently, and he was in the first stages of grief.

Vikki briefed Gomez once Vince was handed over to an officer to take him back to his office.

"I thought he was good for it," Gomez said. "Maybe we'll uncover something later. I'll pull their financial reports. See if you can get Jessica's phone records from your contact at the phone company. And also anything readily available for her sister."

They went back to the squad room to their desks.

For the next two hours, Vikki typed away on her keyboard, finishing the paperwork from Child Protective Services. She started the report for the current case. Soon, a uniform delivered a folder of documents to their table. It didn't take long for Vikki to find records that suggested that maybe Vince Ramsey knew what he was talking about.

"We'll have to bring Jessica's sister in for questioning," Gomez said.

CHAPTER FOURTEEN

Vikki and Gomez arrived at Brie's Nail Salon in Dover Township around 1:30 p.m. It was at the same strip mall that they'd seen Mr. Anderson. The attorney had been involved in an earlier case when a woman Gomez called 'Trophy Wife' had been murdered in a bomb explosion.

A door chime sounded once Vikki pulled open the door, to the smell of perfume and nail polish. A waiting area with two chairs and a coffee table was opposite the entrance.

Vikki counted six nail stations, and none were occupied. On the other side were six pedicure chairs, all empty. Business must be tough.

Three young Asian women, probably in their early to mid-twenties, stood together talking. They all wore matching aprons with Brie's Nail Salon printed on the chest over jeans and tee shirts.

Vikki flashed her badge and introduced herself and Gomez.

The girls drew back and huddled together with narrowed eyes and furrowed foreheads.

Vikki swore and turned to Gomez. "There might be an

issue of labor trafficking here." A report she'd read a while ago about nail salons came to mind. Fellow immigrants exploited new arrivals, most of the time relatives. They got them to the US, confiscated their passport, and trapped them in a job working for them for low wages.

Vikki smiled and put away her badge. Right now, she has a homicide on her hands. Labor trafficking would be for another day.

Gomez raised his hand. "It's okay. We're only looking for Brie Adams?"

The girl closest to Gomez shook her head. "We no see her yet," the girl said in accented English. She pantomimed, raising a cell phone to her ear. "I call. She no reply."

"Hmm, I hope she's okay," Vikki said. "I mean, she should've at least called the police. Her sister made the front page of St. Ives Examiner. She must have seen it."

Just then, the door chime sounded, and the door swung open. A woman strolled in, standing approximately five feet and eight inches tall. She wore a flowing summer dress and held an oversized tote bag of rich, brown leather. She stopped and lowered her sunglasses.

"Brie, Brie, Brie!" the three girls squealed and ran to her.

Finally, Ms. Adams appears, thought Vikki. Apart from her blonde hair cut in a bob, there wasn't much resemblance to her dead sister. Well, Vikki had never seen Jessica when she was alive.

The woman, Brie, shook her head. "Still no customers." It was more of a statement than a question. She sounded like a young college kid.

Vikki walked up to her. "Ms. Adams, I'm Detective Victoria Mattsen from SIPD. My colleague, Detective Mike Gomez."

"Please, call me Brie. Officers, what's this about?"

Gomez tilted his head. "Detectives—you...you haven't heard?"

"Heard what?" Brie asked, eyebrows raised. Her gaze darted from the girls to Gomez and Vikki. "What am I missing here?"

"We call you," one of the girls said. Her voice cracked. She produced a copy of *St. Ives Examiner*.

Brie didn't look at the paper. "Oh, I didn't abandon you. I was with Joe. My phone died."

Vikki cleared her throat. "I'm sorry to inform you, Brie. Someone broke into your sister's home last night and murdered her. Jessica's dead."

The tote left Brie's hand and crashed to the floor. She covered her face with both hands. "No, it can't be true. What happened?"

Gomez led her to the sitting area. "Why don't you sit down." He explained to her what had happened as they walked.

Tears streamed down Brie's face. "But I spoke with her last night."

Vikki sat in the chair next to her. Delivering news like this was part of her job, but it was always challenging. "I'm so sorry."

Her employees hugged each other and sobbed.

For the next few minutes, Brie lowered her head and cried. Her body was racked with sobs. Then she sat up. "Rick!" She turned to Vikki. "My nephew, is he okay?"

"Yes, he's fine," Vikki said.

"He's with Child Protective Services," Gomez said.

"I-I spoke with her last night. She reached out to me...and I blew her off."

This guilty thought triggered another round of sobbing. Vikki tapped her back.

Brie regained her composure. "When can I see Rick? He must be scared."

"Soon," Gomez said. "We have a few questions for you. Do you mind coming down to the station with us?"

"No, not all." Brie got up from the chair and picked up her bag. She rummaged in it and brought out her phone. "It needs to be charged." She laughed, pursed her lips, and tried to be strong. Turning to the girls, she said, "Dung, Diep, Binh. I'll soon be back, okay?"

Vikki guided Brie with her palm on her back. "Let's go."

"What type of questions do you have for me anyway?"

"Nothing out of the ordinary," Vikki said. "Routine questions like, where were you yesterday between eight and nine p.m."

CHAPTER FIFTEEN

At the police station, room one was occupied, so they put Brie in room two. The legs of the chair for the suspect were purposefully made with uneven lengths. This caused perpetual annoying discomfort to the suspect.

"So, which one is the truth?" Gomez asked. "You were in Atlantic City between eight and nine. Or you were in St. Ives?"

Vikki feared they might be barking up the wrong tree. They'd been at this for over an hour. They'd tried to get her to trip up on her story, but she'd been consistent.

"For the last time, I was in St. Ives," Brie said. "Jess doesn't take no for an answer. She would have come looking for me wherever I was. But Atlantic City would be a stretch for her. Any other place she would have come to talk to me about Vince and ruin my evening." She paused after that statement.

Even Vikki felt the impact.

Brie whimpered. Tears rolled down her eyes. "Why are you doing this to me?"

"Brie, we're only doing our job," Vikki said. "We follow

the evidence wherever it points to." She and Gomez were playing the good cop, bad cop. She was the friendly cop.

"Jess and Vince were in love, but she's scared of getting married again. I only wanted to spend a little time with Joe before the new week." Brie paused and drew in a sharp breath. Her gaze shifted from Vikki to Gomez. "Why would I want to murder my sister?"

Gomez didn't miss a beat. "You needed money. You gamble a lot. Your business is not doing well." He picked up one of the reports they'd pulled. "It's on track to close soon unless you turn things around."

Brie shook her head. "We went to Atlantic City to enjoy the beach and have fun at the casino. Not everyone at the casino has a gambling problem. As per my business not doing well, it's all my fault."

Gomez raised an eyebrow. "How?"

"Naivete. A flaw in my research. I can't compete. My prices are reasonable, but my competitors underpay their workers and can afford to charge far less for the services. I'm not pointing fingers, but labor trafficking is a big problem in the nail salon industry."

Vikki nodded. "I think I read that somewhere."

"My business is ethical. Dung, Diep, and Binh are from Vietnam and are here with work visas. I'm now talking to a lawyer to change our business structure. They become equal partners with me. We work our butts off and share the profits."

Gomez threw out his hands. "Ms. Adams, you've told us a lot. But not where you were between eight and nine p.m. My theory is this. You knew your sister had money in her safe. You sent your Joe to the house to break in. But unfortunately, Jessica was home. She came back early. Joe gets her to open the safe, and he cleans it out. But now she'd seen him, so he had no choice but to murder her."

"Stop! Stop! You sound pathetic. It's like you're walking around with a boutonniere, searching for whom to pin it on. After we drove back from Atlantic City, Joe and I had dinner with our marriage counselor at Authentic Italian in Sparta. You can check with the counselor, Ron Madu, and the restaurant. My big sister is paranoid about marriages, and I didn't want her talking me out of mine!" Brie's voice cracked. "I still can't believe she's dead."

The tension in the room crackled like a bowl of Rice Krispies when milk was added.

Brie pointed at Gomez. "Enough of this! I watch *Law and Order*. Either you arrest me now or let me go. And I want my phone call."

Gomez, red-faced, left the room.

Vikki didn't know exactly what to say. She shuffled some of the papers in her hand. "I'm sorry for my partner's style of questioning."

Brie sobbed quietly.

Vikki cleared her throat. "We obtained a copy of your sister's will. She made you the executor of her estate and designated Rick under your care."

"I can't believe Jess is gone. Can I see her?"

Vikki hesitated. "It can be arranged."

There was a knock on the door, and Gomez walked in. He leaned in and whispered in Vikki's ear, "Her alibi checked out. She'd made a reservation last week, and the restaurant confirmed they were there by that time. They sent a video link of the reception area when they checked in."

"I told you so," Brie said. She was not hiding the fact that she'd heard everything.

Gomez turned to her. "I'm sorry, Ms. Adams. I didn't mean to upset you. I spoke with CPS—they'll be releasing Rick to you."

"Thank you," Brie said, and fresh tears came down her cheeks.

Vikki handed her some tissue. "Did Jessica have any enemies? Anyone she butted heads with or hates her guts?"

Brie thought for a moment. "I can only think of her ex— well, they never got divorced. He refused to sign the papers. Jess kicked him out after he repeatedly broke all their marriage vows and occasionally used her and Rick as punching bags. That was five years ago." She cocked her head. "I guess he still has spousal rights."

"What's his name? Do you have an address?"

"I don't have an address. But I think he works for the Big A at their Castleton, New York warehouse. His name is Richard Reid."

Vikki looked up. "He's Rick senior?"

"They were once in love. They didn't start as hostiles," Brie said.

"Makes sense." Vikki gave Brie her card. "Call me if you remember anything."

"Come with me," said Gomez, smiling. "I'll help with the paperwork so you can be reconciled with your nephew as soon as possible." Gomez paused. "It might be temporary since there's a father."

Vikki went back to her desk in the detective squad room. She checked the distance from St. Ives to upstate New York when Gomez flopped onto his seat beside her.

Gomez sighed and said, "What if she had something to do with this?"

"Remember, you taught me to follow the evidence and my gut," Vikki said, her eyes not leaving her screen. "Right now, neither is pointing toward her."

"Right, right."

The phone on Vikki's desk rang. "Mattsen."

"Hello, Detective, Dr. Brandon here."

"Hi."

Dr. Brandon went straight to the point. "Concerning patient Reid, I found something I'd like to share with you and Gomez. Can you come down as soon as possible?"

Vikki held the receiver. No small talk. But wasn't that what she wanted? "Sure, we'll be there." She hung up and then turned to Gomez. "The ME found something."

CHAPTER SIXTEEN

Each time Vikki approached the medical examiner's office, it was no longer business as usual. She had a policy of not having relationships with people she worked with.

Unfortunately, she had rolled in the hay with Dr. Brandon only to have him as the replacement for Dr. Patel, who'd taken a leave of absence for medical reasons.

Even though she liked Brandon, Vikki preferred not to get her cheese from where she got her milk. Any relationship with him was off. Coming to the morgue was like passing your high school crush in the hallway.

A technician in scrubs worked by a shelf in the corner of the morgue.

Dr. Brandon wore a white tee shirt and blue scrubs over it, complementing his massive biceps. He had shoe covers over his shoes and no other protective gear. He was not doing any autopsies.

Vikki was checking him out when he caught her looking. Heat rushed to her cheeks. She glanced away.

"Thanks for coming so fast," Brandon said.

Gomez turned all serious. "I did not."

Brandon chuckled. "Okay, you're here. Follow me." He walked over to a steel table with a body and a white sheet draped over it. He slipped on blue latex gloves and moved the sheet to the chest.

It was Jessica Reid, scrubbed clean of blood and makeup. She appeared peaceful in death. Vikki remembered that her sister wanted to see her.

"Once I brought her back and examined her with brighter lights, I found this scar behind her neck." Brandon called out to the technician, "Pete, I need some help over here."

Together, they tilted the body to the side. Dr. Brandon pointed out two dark scars on the back of the victim's neck.

"Are those fang marks," Gomez said. "A snake bit her?"

"I thought the same, too," Brandon said.

Vikki exhaled. "What made them?"

Brandon and the tech returned Jessica to her back.

Brandon nodded at the tech. "Thank you."

"Anytime, Doc." The tech walked away.

"I think she was immobilized with a Taser. I'm waiting for her tox screen."

Vikki's pulse beat faster. "What else did you find?"

He pointed at her shoulder. "There's a tiny dark spot, which might not mean anything. Once I get the tox screen result, it will shed light on what, exactly, we're dealing with."

"When do you expect it back?" Gomez asked.

"I put a rush on it. Hopefully in the next twenty-four hours."

CHAPTER SEVENTEEN

Vikki walked into Shop Rite, got a cart, and traveled from aisle to aisle, searching for baked ziti ingredients. She craved it and wanted to make it from scratch—pasta, minced beef, parsley, basil, et cetera.

Before leaving work, Gomez glanced at her screen and said, "You're not thinking of driving to Castleton, New York, are you?"

"I just want a rough idea of how far it is before evidence demands we go there." Vikki had pointed at the screen. "It's like a three-hour drive from here."

"Exactly what I'm saying. Do you think he drove three hours to St. Ives, murdered his estranged wife, then drove back? What's his motive after five years?"

Vikki had shrugged. "We agreed money was stolen. Mallory knows his stuff. That's an excellent motive, especially when you don't have any. Then there are the spousal rights. Plus, he can claim Richard Junior for tax benefits. Even though Jessica had a will, if he sued, they'd be wrapped in litigation that might take years to resolve."

Gomez had nodded. "Then their lawyers would advise

them to find common ground. So out of thin air, he pulls out some settlement. And lives happily ever after."

Vikki had glanced up at him and winked. "That is, assuming we don't get him for murder."

"Find out where he lives," Gomez had said. "If he's living large, I'll rule him out. If he's in a trailer park, we must find out what he was doing between eight and nine last night."

Vikki already knew he was not living large. The company he worked for had its headquarters in Seattle, where the big shots lived. But Reid was in New York.

She'd searched the DMV database and found Richard Reid of Castleton, NY. Her eyes had almost popped out of their sockets. "Gomez, you won't believe this. Mr. Reid does live in a trailer park."

The words that flew out of Gomez's mouth would make a nun blush and a high schooler laugh.

Vikki smiled as she remembered. She was pulled out of her reverie when a woman shopping next to her glanced at her, then exited the aisle hurriedly.

Vikki found herself in the magazine aisle. She noticed the newspaper with a picture of Jessica. The headline read: SINGLE MOTHER, MURDERED.

Despite the tragedy, she smiled. *Angie does love her headlines*. Vikki made herself a promise—she wouldn't rest until whoever had murdered Jessica Reid was brought to justice.

Motherhood is tough, and not all mothers are the same. Vikki had a crappy mother. But when mothers do the right thing, and some bastard ends their life because of greed, they must pay.

CHAPTER EIGHTEEN

The sound came again like rain on a window. Vikki opened one eye, then the other. She was in her Explorer. She'd drifted in and out of sleep. Had she spent the night in her car?

Water splashed on her passenger-side window with a loud *vroom* sound.

Vikki rested her hand on the butt of her Glock nestled in the belt holster on her waist. She glanced around her vicinity. Her car was parked across the street from a trailer park with mostly RVs. It all came back to her in a rush. She was in Castleton, New York.

Water struck the passenger-side window again, and Vikki realized it was a sprinkler on a rhythmic cycle. She checked the time on the clock on her dash. It was just after five in the morning. Was it too early to knock on someone's door? Oh yes, it was. She could answer that one.

The trailer park was beginning to wake up. A few cars had driven out. She would wait until six, then search for Richard Reid.

Vikki smelled French vanilla and reached for her coffee in the cup holder. She twirled the liquid and took a sip. The cold coffee dregs would have been revolting. But the taste was welcome, better than their break room mud anyway. She drank it all and put the cup down.

Her mind drifted to last night at the grocery store. She'd bought the newspaper and read Angie's article in the car. Then she'd decided not to do any cooking and drive up to New York. She'd contemplated calling Gomez. It would only lead to delays. He'd go into a lengthy debate about whether to come or not.

After a one-hour nap, she'd showered and dressed. On her way, she'd bought a cup of coffee and sandwiches from Dunkin and hit the road.

Vikki felt that something was off. Then she realized that the water hitting her window had stopped. She turned, and her heart dropped into the pit of her stomach.

A man's face peered into her car from the outside.

Heart pounding, she reached for her gun.

The man wasn't watching her. He was focused on the newspaper on the seat. It meant one thing. Vikki put the gun away and took the newspaper. Only then did the man glance up, his eyes wide.

Vikki grabbed her black jacket from the back seat. She got out of the car and slipped it on as the man walked around the car to her.

"Good morning," he said. His voice was deep, hoarse, like someone that'd just woken up. He adjusted his red robe, covered the blue pajamas, then tightened the belt. "New Jersey plates. Can I see the newspaper?"

"Sure." Vikki reached into the car, retrieved the paper, and gave it to him. "I'm Detective Victoria Mattsen from—"

"St. Ives Police Department," said the man, finishing the sentence. "I came to investigate why you were parked in front of my house for the past three hours."

Vikki stared at him. The black hair and Will Smith's ears were unmistakable.

"Mr. Reid." Vikki glanced at the trailer park and back at him. "I thought you lived over there."

"I used to." He smiled. "Now I own the trailer park. It's more of an RV parking ground. Plus, the property you're parked in front of." He explained to her how the property was like a lottery ticket. "I saw the potential once Big A started talking of locating a fulfillment warehouse here, and I took a gamble."

The fact that Mr. Reid was doing well put a dent in Vikki and Gomez's theory of financial gain being the motive if it was him who'd killed Jessica.

Mr. Reid finished reading the front page and let out a sigh. "Jessica was murdered? What a shame. That must be why CPS left a message on my phone to call them."

"I'm so sorry for your loss," Vikki said.

"Don't be. It's not my loss. We've been estranged for five years now. You drove all night to inform me of Jessica's death?"

Vikki nodded. "I also wanted to know where you were between eight and nine on Sunday night."

He pursed his lips and nodded. "Of course. Easy, I was at work at the Big A warehouse on Roosevelt Street."

It occurred to Vikki that he might have done the same thing she'd done. Drove to St. Ives, then back to Castleton. The next remark out of his mouth snuffed out that thought.

"Everyone saw me. I was the shift manager. A phone call would have saved you the trip."

"Is there anyone you think would have wanted to hurt Jessica?"

He shook his head. "No."

For the first time, Vikki saw sadness in his eyes.

"Jess can be pushy sometimes...I don't know."

Vikki gave him her card. "Please call me if you remember anything that might help the investigation." She turned to open her car door.

"And the boy?"

Vikki let out a breath. "Your son is fine. Brie has custody."

The crow's feet around Mr. Reid's eyes softened as if a huge boulder had been lifted off his shoulder. "He's not my son. I had a vasectomy. After five years, I couldn't bear raising another man's child."

"Honey, I have your coffee," said a female voice.

A blonde of college age stood in front of the door to Reid's house in a man's shirt. She raised a steaming mug.

Reid waved. "Coming." He turned to Vikki. "Thanks for driving up here."

Vikki left and drove to Big A's office at Roosevelt Street. She introduced herself and showed her badge. The secretary was very cooperative. She confirmed that Mr. Reid was there in a meeting at those times.

"I can send you a link to a time-stamped video of the meeting after I clear it with security," the secretary said.

Vikki wrote down her SIPD email. "I'd appreciate that."

Before heading back to New Jersey, Vikki stopped at a McDonald's. She used the bathroom, replenished her coffee, and got breakfast. Sitting and eating in her car, she queried the all-knowing Google about vasectomy failures. One in two of every thousand men. Was Mr. Reid one of those men?

Then she read that it took about three months after a vasectomy to be free of sperm. It was still possible for a woman to get pregnant three months after her partner had got the procedure. With those ears, the apple didn't fall far from the tree.

CHAPTER NINETEEN

"I can't believe you went to see Mr. Reid without me," Gomez said.

Vikki hung her jacket on her chair. "It was one of those moments of madness. I got in the car and started driving."

"You've already covered a lot for the day, and it's only nine-thirty. Is he our guy?"

Vikki shook her head. "His alibi checked out. The trailer park we thought he lived in, he owns. It's more of an RV parking area. The fulfillment center he works for hires seasonal workers now and then, especially at Christmas. So, he's already making money. Then during those seasons, his income explodes."

"So that eliminates our motive," Gomez said. "What about if he did it for revenge or something."

"I doubt it. He claims Richard Junior is not his son, but the resemblance exists. He was so relieved when I told him Brie had custody. I think he didn't want to be responsible for any child."

"Well, CPS will have to deal with it if he wants the boy to

stay with Brie," Gomez said. "So technically, we're back to square one." He took a sip of his coffee.

"Only technically. We've eliminated people, so the pool is narrowing."

"Who else is in the pool?"

"We have to find out who those honeymooners are?"

"Why waste time? When they left town, Ms. Reid was still alive. They could be in California for all I care."

Vikki sat in her chair and made a steeple with her hand. "Have the computer guys been able to get to her computer yet?"

"I don't think so. I'll go over and scare them into action."

"We never recovered her phone," Vikki said. "I bet it's somewhere in the house. There must be text messages and emails with the guest's information."

"What if we used the old-fashioned way of observation? Let's talk to the boyfriend again. Maybe there are things he remembers now that he didn't then."

Vikki doubted it. "He would rather put the whole incident behind him than continue to dwell on it. Do you have his number?"

Gomez opened drawers on his table and looked at folders. "I should have it somewhere."

Vikki typed in 'Ramsey Publications' in her browser and hit 'enter.' Vince's place of work came up. She tapped on it, and soon it rang on the other end. "Don't worry, Gomez. I have it. Google is becoming a major part of my research."

"Hello, Ramsey Publications. Liz speaking, how can I help you?"

Liz's voice was pleasant and bubbly.

"This is Detective Victoria Mattsen of SIPD. May I speak with Mr. Vince Ramsey?"

"Just a moment," Liz said.

A few seconds later, Mr. Ramsey's said, "Detective, this is a surprise." He sounded cold.

"We need your help. Just—"

"You need my help," said Mr. Ramsey, cutting her off.

His breathing came through the phone. Vikki was sure he believed they were hard on him for no reason. "Mr. Ramsey, we're trying to find out who did this and bring them to justice. I just returned from Castleton, New York, to see Jessica's ex. We're following every lead. Did you see the couple she dropped off at the train station?"

There was a long pause.

"Mr. Ramsey? Are you there?"

He sighed again. "Yes, I did see them. All I remember is that the woman was as tall as the man. I have difficulty describing things, a type of mind dyslexia. I'm sorry."

"Mr. Ramsey, anything you can remember will be appreciated. We have artists in the building who can do more with less. We can come to you, or you can come to us, and it won't take any time. With a sketch, it becomes easier for the public to help."

"Detective, sorry, I can't help you." There was finality in his voice. "I have to go, and please keep me updated."

"Sure. Thanks for your time." Vikki placed her phone on the desk.

"He won't even talk to an artist?" Gomez asked. "Maybe he's somehow connected to them."

Vikki hadn't thought of that. "Tell me more."

"There isn't more. Just a thought. You'll be the first to know if I flesh anything out."

"I think I'll return to the crime scene," Vikki said. "Her phone wasn't accounted for. It must hold a trove of information."

Gomez shook his head. "I went through the whole house and didn't find it. The CS investigators did, too. No stone was left unturned. What we didn't find was the cat, Kitty. Rick said it's brown."

"Okay, I'll go take a second look. The second pair of eyes might be all it takes." Vikki tidied her desk and got up. "Did Santiago get back to you?"

"No, was she supposed to?"

"I'd asked her to question the neighbors that night."

"Oh boy," Gomez said. "I can see McClane's interfering fingers all over this. I'll follow up with her."

CHAPTER TWENTY

Vikki sat in her car and tried to put herself in the shoes of the murderer. How had they got here? Either the person drove, or someone dropped them off. That would mean an accomplice. From all indications, there had only been one attacker inside.

She reached behind in the car seat and picked up a crime scene overall she'd brought from the squad room. She put it on, then gloves and booties from her glove compartment.

With her protective clothing in place, she approached the stairs of the Greek revival, the early morning sun warm on her face. The sound of a lawn mower and the smell of cut grass immediately hit her. A neighbor was already taking care of business early. She thought of Castleton—no regrets about going there. That was one suspect out of the way for now.

The yellow police tape across the door was intact. And so were the ones on the windows facing the front porch. Vikki peeled off the one across the entrance. It was more of a deterrent than an unbreachable barrier. Violators would be prosecuted for tampering with a crime scene.

The killer must have rung the bell. Vikki reached for it

and froze. Her heartbeat galloped faster. It was a Ring door-bell—and this one had a video camera. How in the world had they missed this?

Adrenaline rushed through her. Somewhere in the Ring cloud was the image of the killer.

Hands shaking, she unzipped the overall and extracted her phone. She tapped the screen and called Gomez.

"Mattsen! You just left the office. You solved the crime already?"

Vikki ignored his dig. "The bell on the door doubles as a video camera. The killer's image must be saved somewhere. Any way of getting access to a customer's video footage with Ring?"

"Well, the customer always has access to the videos through their account," Gomez said. "They can access it from their phone or tablet. There's an app for that."

Vikki groaned. "We don't have her phone. That brings us back to square one again. Would it be on her seized comput-er?" She thought for a moment. "Any way of getting the footage from Ring? Do we need a warrant to get them to share data?"

"Slow down. Too many questions—let me ask around. Hold on."

Vikki waited. Bits and pieces of conversation from the squad room filtered down the line. She hoped he would have good news. She brought out the key to the door from her pocket and was reaching for the keyhole when Gomez spoke.

"Ring has over two thousand enforcement agencies enrolled in its Neighbors Public Service platform. I'm sure we'll be there. Knock on wood."

The sound of his knuckle on the desk reached Vikki.

"If we're already enrolled, which I think we are, easy-peasy, we can request footage from them."

"What if we're not there?" Vikki said. "The more time we

delay, the colder the trail of the perp gets." A shaky breath shuddered out of her. "If only we had her phone."

"I tell you what. Why don't you continue with what you're doing? I'll put in the request for data access. It's like the lottery—you can't win if you don't play."

"Thanks, Gomez." Vikki hung up and turned the key. She opened the door and entered, closing it behind her.

The place was just as they'd left it early Monday morning with its French Empire-style furniture. She flicked on the light switch and listened. Right away, a scratching noise came from the kitchen. *Do they have mice?* She headed in that direction.

The sound stopped when she stepped onto the kitchen's wooden floor. Then it resumed, more frantic. It was coming from a cabinet with a door. Vikki was at a loss for what to do. Then she remembered Gomez mentioning a cat was missing.

She yanked the cabinet door open.

A brown furry object shot out. Vikki yelped and jumped. It was the missing cat. It ran into a barstool, then dashed into the living room.

The smell hit Vikki, and she gagged. She pinched her nose and peered into the cabinet. Inside was a mixture of cat poop, urine, and cat food pellets from a ripped bag.

She saw something shiny and leaned in. It was the unmistakable shape of a cellphone in a polished yellowish case. Vikki ripped off some paper towels from the counter and grabbed it.

She wiped it and tried to turn it on. It wouldn't—probably dead. She placed it in an evidence bag, then called Gomez.

"Vikki! I'm still working on it."

"Gomez. Guess what the cat dragged in."

CHAPTER TWENTY-ONE

Vikki kept the phone in the evidence bag and plugged her charger into it. She then set off for the PD. When the phone lit up, she almost swerved excitedly into oncoming traffic. Like most phones, it was password protected. She felt they were going to break the case.

At the office, she cut across the detective squad room en route to the forensic computer lab.

She dodged some detectives rushing off to what she overheard on the dispatch as a bad house fire—with fatalities.

"Vikki," Gomez said and jumped to his feet. He followed her. He was always looking for an opportunity to make fun of their young resident civilian computer geeks, whom he'd dubbed 'the apostles.'

Vikki barged into the computer lab without knocking. The smell of stale pizza hit her. In the corner was the culprit, a small stack of pizza boxes.

On a table from one end of the room to the other were three blinking computer monitors and monitors with dead screens. Empty cans of Red Bull littered the table, plus phones and tablets in different stages of disassembling.

One of the duo Gomez called 'the apostles,' James Madden, was rocking to music. Next to him was a steaming cup of coffee. He didn't glance up. He probably had on noise-canceling headphones.

"My God, it smells like a frat house here," Gomez said. He walked over and tapped James on the shoulder.

James looked up. His eyes widened, then he smiled. He removed his headphone and raised it. "Noise-canceling. I didn't hear you come in."

Vikki pushed the phone at him. "I need this phone unlocked right now."

The plastic crinkled as James took it. "Hmm, do you have a warrant?"

"No," Vikki said. "It belongs to a homicide victim. Your Fourth and Fifth Amendment rights generally end when you do."

Gomez inhaled and exhaled sharply. "Information in the phone will lead to identifying the killer."

James was quiet for a moment. He placed the evidence on the table, reached for a box of latex gloves, and pulled out two. "I'll try, but you'll still need a warrant if I can't." He slipped them on, then unzipped the bag.

"Why?" Vikki and Gomez asked at the same time.

"Because today, at this point, it might change in the future. Only a judge can order Apple to unlock the phone."

"Why?" Vikki and Gomez asked again in unison.

James eyed them. "We are searching for evidence against someone else, the perp, whose Fourth Amendment rights are intact. He's still protected him from unreasonable search."

Gomez rolled his eyes. "Did they teach you that at Stanford?"

James pulled the phone out and gagged. "What's that smell?"

Vikki looked away, massaging her neck.

Gomez sniffed. "Cat shit. Smells better than your office."

"Jesus," James said in a squeaky voice. "Come back in an hour."

They left but checked on him every twenty minutes. After an hour, he was still unable to unlock it.

Vikki let out an exasperated breath. "So close, and yet so far."

"Where is the other apostle?" Gomez asked. "Maybe he has the magic touch."

"John is off today," said James. "I'm so sorry. You'll probably need that warrant."

Vikki inhaled, then exhaled, dragging her shoulders down. They were this close to solving the crime. Now they needed to get a warrant which was very unlikely because of walking over the rights of a murderer.

Jessica Reid had been murdered in cold blood. She deserved justice.

The solution came to Vikki like a light beam from a lighthouse guiding a ship on a foggy night.

"I know who to ask. Give me the phone."

"Where are you going?"

"I'll be right back." Vikki took the phone and left. Her heart rattled in her rib cage, similar to a deer trying to escape a house it had broken into. She took a deep breath, muttering a mantra as she exhaled. "Whatever it takes."

CHAPTER TWENTY-TWO

Twenty minutes later, she was back in the computer lab, and Jessica's phone was hooked up to one of the monitors. Vikki, Gomez, and James sat in front of the screen, watching.

Gomez chuckled. "James, do you have popcorn?"

Nobody else found it funny.

A female mechanical voice said, "Turn right on Main Street." This had been going on every few minutes.

James reached for the phone. "I'll turn that map voice off."

Vikki grabbed his hand. "Don't you dare." She said each word slowly.

John drew back, startled. "Okay."

The image on the monitor showed Jessica at her door. She opened it and stepped in. She looked like an older version of her sister. The camera now showed Jessica's car and the house across the street.

"Should we speed it up?" Gomez asked.

"No, we don't want to miss anything," Vikki said. Her pulse raced faster and faster, seeing Jessica alive than when she'd gone downstairs to the morgue more than twenty minutes ago.

She'd walked with her chin high, shoulders back, and chest out. She'd hoped that Dr. Brandon had gone to respond to the fire announced by dispatch.

Vikki had used her access key card to enter the morgue. It would register somewhere. It didn't matter. She had access to be there. Vikki had walked over to the computer where the morgue records were kept. She had a good idea of where the password was. Otherwise, she would have to open every drawer.

Her leg had bumped the table, the mouse moved, and the screen came alive. Someone had exited the program in a hurry. The login window to the mortuary management software had been on screen with the username and password already filled. She'd clicked enter, and she was in.

Vikki let out a breath. So far, so good. She'd clicked on occupancy, and a dropdown window showed rows of names. She'd found what she was looking for.

Jessica Reid, 32, Female, MC 14.

There were other columns, but all she needed was the cabinet number. She'd snapped on gloves and walked over to the refrigerator. She'd seen Dr. Patel retrieve a body from the morgue many times.

She located MC 14 and pulled. The naked body had appeared inch by inch. Without looking at Jessica's face, she'd lifted her hand and reached into her pocket for the phone. It wasn't there.

Pulse racing, she'd looked around, then saw it on the computer table. She'd rushed over and retrieved it. Vikki had placed Jessica's thumb at the bottom center of the screen. Nothing happened. She'd tried the index finger.

Nothing.

"What the?"

The morgue had been freezing, but sweat had trickled down the middle of her back. She'd tried the middle finger, and the phone had come to life.

Vikki let out a huge breath. She'd felt herself starting to fall and caught herself. She'd slipped the phone into her back pocket, tucked Jessica's arm in, and pushed her back in. She'd brought the phone out, and the screen had been dark.

"No, no, no." Jessica had tapped the screen furiously. The homepage had come back on.

She'd activated the map app, selected home, and muted the volume. The phone wouldn't go to the lock screen if the map were active.

"Turn right on Main Street."

The mechanical voice brought Jessica out of her reverie. The image on the screen got darker and darker. "What's happening?"

"These are snapshots," James said. "The video is motion activated. It captures snapshots when nothing is moving."

Around 8:05, a beam of light swept through the driveway.

"Here comes the killer," Gomez said, leaning forward.

A man with a baseball cap approached from the left side, suggesting he was a passenger. He angled his head so his face was never on camera. He reached for the bell. The time stamp was 8:10. Jessica appeared on the screen and smiled. They spoke for a bit, then she invited the man in. The only sound in the room was the humming of computer hard drives.

About ten minutes later, the front door opened, and the man came out. He carried a bag. He went out of camera range. Then the light beam died off.

James exhaled. "Wow."

For a while, nothing happened. Then, another beam of light swept through. A boy ran toward the camera.

"Rick," Vikki muttered.

Moments later, a woman dashed for the stairs. About ten minutes later, flashing lights as the police arrived.

"Can you rewind it to when the killer approached?"

"Sure."

Vikki paid attention, trying to see the unseeable. But the man hid his face.

"He knew what he was doing," said Gomez. "Like he had done it before. I think the killer was the passenger. Looks like pros. They came in, murdered, stole, and left."

"Wait, didn't Mallory say something similar happened in New Hampshire?" Vikki brought out her phone and called Mallory.

The Chief of SIPD CSU confirmed and gave Vikki the town in New Hampshire where an Airbnb landlord had been murdered. Ten minutes later, Vikki was on the phone with Detective Matt Johnston of the Harcourt Towns Police Department.

"It was a couple," Detective Johnston said. "They rented a room. They were dropped off at the station by the owner. However, they returned, murdered the owner, and emptied her safe. The MO is similar, but our culprits are both doing life. You probably have another couple in your area. Maybe a copycat duo."

Vikki thanked him and hung up. She described to Gomez what Matt Johnston had said to her.

"Our perps might still be around," Gomez said.

They thanked James, dropped the phone at forensics, and returned to the squad office.

"We should go to the train station and check their surveillance videos," Vikki said.

Gomez nodded. That video was close. If only he'd shown his face.

Vikki felt drained—not sure the next step to take. Then someone called her name. It was Officer Acosta.

"Hey, Acosta, thanks for bringing in Rick and Sally. It was a busy night."

"No problem. Detective Santiago gave me this for you." He handed Vikki a piece of paper ripped from a notepad. "It's from that night, too. She said one of the neighbors provided the information."

"Who?"

Acosta swallowed. "She said all the information is in there."

"Where's Santiago?"

"At the fire scene. I have to go."

"Thanks," Vikki said. She had a feeling Acosta had forgotten to hand it over. She read the note. A midsize white SUV drove in twice to the house. "Small white SUV?" she mumbled. She remembered a white Compass had been parked behind the red BMW the night of the murder.

"Anything important?" Gomez asked.

"I can't say for sure. In number twenty-five, a Mary Lippincott across saw a white SUV twice in the driveway."

"Yeah, it was there. Belonged to the play date's mother. Let's see if there's any luck with St. Ives' train station."

CHAPTER TWENTY-THREE

Vikki and Gomez arrived at the train station just after a train had left, leaving a desolate platform and lobby in its wake. They went to the ticket booth, and Gomez asked the middle-aged woman in it who was in charge of security.

"Why do you want to know?" the woman asked.

"I'm sorry," Gomez said. He showed her his badge and introduced himself. "That's my partner, Detective Mattsen."

"You should have said so. That will be Dave you want to see." She pointed across the hall. "Knock on that door. Explain who you are and show your badge. And ask for Dave. I saw him earlier with his lunch bag. He should be back by now."

Ten minutes later, they stood in a cramped office the size of a closet, watching surveillance videos. The odor of aged paper and old files filled the enclosure. Dave must have eaten something with red onions for lunch, which didn't help. Gomez explained why they were there.

"As long as they came through here, they are on our videos," said Dave Smith, a fifty-something man with a quiet voice. "Who exactly are you searching for?"

"A man and woman. Dropped off around five or six p.m. on Sunday," Vikki said.

Dave chuckled. "Good luck." Then he cocked his head. "You know, traffic is slow on Sundays. This might be quick. Perhaps your luck is already changing. We'll start with camera shots from the entrance and then look at those inside." He glanced over his shoulder at Vikki and Gomez. "I'll drive. You two keep your eyes peeled." He typed a few commands on the keyboard. "I'll start at four p.m. Sunday."

Dave sped up the video. It was black and white and grainy. To Vikki, it could've been a Charlie Chaplin movie without the comic relief.

Beside Vikki, Gomez was pulling at his tie, adjusting the collar of his shirt. It wasn't hot in the closet, but it wasn't comfortable inside the tiny space.

Cars came and went. Around 5:30 p.m., the familiar twin-kidney grille of the German machine pulled up. Vikki's pulse picked up a notch.

"Wow, that's them," Gomez said, pointing.

Vikki watched with trepidation. The passenger-side door opened. A woman got out. Then a man got out from the back. The woman's blonde hair reached her shoulders. Her tee shirt and jeans suggested she was not in a hurry. The man's outfit was the male version of the woman's. The main difference in their appearance was his hair color which was black compared to her blonde.

"That must be them," Dave said with a laugh.

Gomez nodded. "How did you know."

"You two suddenly stopped breathing."

Vikki exhaled noisily through her nose. On the screen, Jessica ran around the front of the car with her hand stretched out and a big smile. She hugged and kissed the couple on the cheeks one after the other.

Jessica must have popped the trunk because she raised it

and brought two hand luggage-size suitcases. They hugged again.

Vikki couldn't stomach what she was seeing. All that love. Her astonishment shifted to rage.

Dave tilted his head up. "They murdered her? They could pass as good friends." He shook his head. "That's the worst type."

The next shot showed them inside the station. They seemed to be smiling at the camera.

"Freeze it!" Vikki said.

Dave raised his eyebrows. "You like that? Let's see if I can make it any better." He attacked the keyboard, selecting the head and shoulder shots. The image became larger and sharper.

Vikki could hardly breathe. "That's good!" She fished out her cell phone and snapped a picture of the couple on the screen. She saved it to her phone.

Gomez brought out his phone. "Are you sending it to James for face ID?" He woke his phone with a tap on the screen. He swiped, tapped then pressed the phone against his ear.

"You bet," Vikki said and sent the photo to James.

"Hello, James. Gomez here. Check your email. Mattsen sent you a picture of a couple. Please run it through facial recognition ASAP. Let us know as soon as you have a match."

Vikki put away her phone. She touched the handle of her gun, brushed her hair behind her ears, and rubbed her palms together. Adrenaline coursed through her. She was excited. "Let's go back to the squad room. I think—"

The sound of an incoming text cut Vikki off.

Gomez's phone rang at the same time.

The text message was from James. It showed two names —Doug Penne and Anna Ford. Vikki said the names out loud.

"Got it," Gomez said.

Vikki took her eyes away from her phone and turned to Gomez. "We have to run." She squeezed Dave's shoulder. "Thanks so much. We owe you."

"Glad I was of service."

Vikki headed for the door. Let's pull their financial statement. It will help locate them if it shows the last place they used a credit card." She sighed, shaking her head. They could be far gone by now. "It might be Beijing."

"Doug Penne and Anna Ford," said Gomez, his phone pressed to his ear. "I'm on it."

They were already getting feedback by the time they got to the car.

"What!" Gomez shouted into his phone.

Vikki inserted her seat belt, then glanced at Gomez.

"They're still in the area? At the mall?" Gomez said, an incredulous look on his face. He turned to Vikki. "Doug Penn's credit card was used at the food court at St. Ives' mall ten minutes ago. Then at the movie theater five minutes ago. They are about to see a movie at the mall."

"Put out a BOLO! Send uniforms to the theater. They should wait for us and not engage the suspects."

Vikki pushed the button to lower her window. She grabbed a magnetic strobe light from under a pile of newspapers in the backseat and stuck it on the roof of her car. She plugged it into the auxiliary car outlet.

"Bonnie and Clyde, here we come," Vikki said.

CHAPTER TWENTY-FOUR

Vikki and Gomez arrived at the movie theater with their lights on. About four or five police cruisers were already in place with flashing red and blue lights. Vikki saw a problem. Should they evacuate first and storm the movie theater? Or go in stealth?

These questions rolled around her head like corn in a microwave about to start popping.

Then her cell phone rang.

A call had been rerouted to her. An off-duty policeman, Officer Ed Thomas. He worked theater security as a second job.

"Detective Mattsen, I saw them go into Theater Three. I have their seat numbers, too. The movie should start in the next few minutes."

Vikki thought fast.

She was out of the car, taking long strides with Gomez behind her. "Stay put. You're our eyes and ears. We don't want to cause panic. Detective Gomez and I will stroll in. How do we recognize you?"

"I have on a yellow vest that says Theater Security."

"Good. See you in a minute."

Vikki checked her Glock. It was ready. She tucked it back in. She recognized some of the uniforms by the door. She said to the one closest to her, "Quietly stop anyone from coming in."

To the next one, she said, "Evacuate the lobby to the kitchen once Gomez and I enter Theater Three."

She stepped in, and the smell of butter and popcorn enveloped her. Officer Thomas was easy to spot. He acknowledged her presence with a raised fist, his gaze fixed on the entrance of Theater Three.

Vikki strolled over. "Officer Thomas, what's their seat number?"

"G22 and G23."

Vikki once had a summer job at the movies and knew about the seating arrangement. You enter at C. The area with space for wheelchairs splits the theater into two unequal parts.

"You know how to get in from the back door?"

Officer Thomas nodded.

"Get two more officers and enter from the back exit at K6 and K5. Gomez and I will approach from the bottom, coming up, pretending to be searching for seats. We'll take them and exit from the back."

"Roger that," Officer Thomas said and headed toward the Employees Only door. He motioned to two officers and led the way to the back of Theater Three.

Vikki turned to Gomez. "Show time."

They went up a short ramp, made a right, and started up the seating area. The lights hadn't been dimmed yet as commercials were still being shown.

She recited the alphabet in her mind, glancing to her left and up, checking off the rows. Doug Penne and Anna Ford occupied the first two seats in G row. They were preoccupied feeding each other popcorn from a large bowl on Doug's lap.

Behind them, Officer Thomas and the others were in position.

Vikki's heart pounded like a jackhammer. They had the element of surprise. But something might go wrong. She followed the alphabet carved into the stairs, a letter on each step. Vikki stopped at G. She was filled with loathing for the couple.

Doug Penne must have felt her eyes on him. He turned to Vikki and smiled.

Vikki had one hand on the butt of her Glock and her badge in her left hand.

Doug's smile faded. "What the...?"

The rest of the officers came down. The game was up.

"Doug Penne—Anna Ford, you're both under arrest for the murder of Jessica Reid!" Vikki said.

Vikki read them their rights. They did not resist. They cuffed them and whisked them away like lambs being led to the slaughter.

CHAPTER TWENTY-FIVE

Vikki and Gomez waited at their desks in the squad room as Doug Penne and Anna Ford were processed. Their mug shots and fingerprints went into the system.

Captain Levin was all smiles. "Make it stick, Mattsen. I'll be at the window."

Because the evidence they had on camera from Ms. Reid's home was of a man, they started with Anna Ford, hoping she would incriminate them further.

Anna Ford was thirty-four and soft-spoken. She could've been a kindergarten teacher or guidance counselor at a school. By the time they'd spent an hour questioning her, doubt had crept into Vikki's mind. Anna answered the questions like someone recalling and then responding with facts.

"Where were you between eight and nine p.m. on Sunday?"

Anna frowned, then brightened up. "Yes, we were at Times Square. Then dinner at Olive Garden after we arrived."

Vikki was at a loss. Anna's reply was consistent. There was no prelude to murder in her story. They ended the interview and went to the next room to talk to Doug Penne.

Vikki and Gomez sat opposite Penne in interview one. She asked Santiago to contact Olive Garden and confirm if they were there.

Gomez read Doug Penne his rights, then offered him some refreshments. "Coffee, water, or soda?"

Penn declined. They'd transported them in different patrol cars to the station. Now the moment of truth—to see if their stories held up.

Doug Penne glared at Vikki. "Detective, you said Jessica was dead. Then you guys kept me waiting for an hour. I don't know whose idea of a joke this is, but it's no longer funny."

Vikki's insides tightened. Was she wrong? They had not resisted arrest. They had complied all the way.

"Look around you," Gomez said. "This is St. Ives Police Station. It's no joke."

"Where's Anna?"

Vikki was tired. She stared at Penne, contemplating what to say to him.

Penne's face turned red. His nostrils flared. "If anything happens to her, I'll—"

"You'll do what? Snuff me out with a blow to the head, as you did to Jessica Reid?"

Doug drew back. "What? Jessica's dead?" He sat back and covered his mouth with his hand. "Oh my God," he said in a low voice. "What happened?"

"Where were you between eight and nine p.m. on Sunday?"

Penne cleared his throat. "Jess dropped us off at the station."

"Which station?" Gomez asked.

"St. Ives train station, around five-thirty. We got our tickets and went to Penn Station in New York. Took about an hour and thirty-six minutes. From there, we went to Times Square."

"Did anybody see you?" Gomez asked.

"Did anybody see us at the mall?" Penne said. "People saw us, and so did security and tourist cameras. It won't be hard to prove we were there."

Vikki thought it was time to change direction. "How did you meet Jessica?"

Penne's face lit up. "She's an interior decorator and an avid antique collector. I don't know if you've visited her house, it's amazing. We meet on an online site—Trash n Treasure. It's an online community for people who enjoy garage sales, estate sales, and garbage diving, looking for things to buy, rescue, use, or resell."

"Where did you get married?" Gomez asked.

"In Vegas."

Vikki raised an eyebrow. "And you're honeymooning in St. Ives?"

"That wasn't the plan," Penne said. "There was a big estate sale in Saddle River. It clashed with our honeymoon plans. We would have missed it, but Jess...Jessica insisted on hosting us."

"Okay, you arrived on Friday," Vikki said. "Went for the estate sale, then what happened?"

Penne glanced from Vikki to Gomez. "We didn't make it to the estate sale."

Vikki drew in a sharp breath and exhaled through her nose.

"We arrived late because we missed our connecting flight. But we were excited when Jess showed us what she bought, a seventeenth-century ivory necklace from Benin. She was more interested in French Empire-era art and bought it because she had us in mind. We offered to buy it from her."

"At a profit?" said Gomez.

"No. The same price she paid for it. It was listed for fifteen thousand dollars. She paid ten."

Vikki cocked her head. "How did she get a five-thousand-dollar reduction?"

Penn shrugged. "She offered cash. It still works in getting you a bargain. Some bargain hunters like Jessica still carry bundles of cash around."

Vikki now got the picture of where the cash in the safe had come from. So they had to pay her back in cash.

Penne continued. "We went to the bank, withdrew money, and gave it to her. That was the only time we left her house."

"Nice story," Gomez said. "Who can collaborate it?"

Penne was quiet for a moment. "A friend of hers came with us. You can ask her. She's about five-six or seven. She didn't talk much, but she had flaming red hair. I have a picture on my phone if you can bring my phone back."

Vikki's pulse was racing. Her fears were being realized. Just then, her phone vibrated in her pocket. The ME was calling. She stood and answered. "Mattsen."

"Hi, the tox screen result is back. This will help your case."

Adrenaline pumped through her body. If my heart beats any faster, thought Vikki, I'll end up in the hospital as a patient.

CHAPTER TWENTY-SIX

Vikki stepped out into the hall, her phone pressed to her ear. A lot was happening all at once.

Gomez was right behind her. "I'll go get his phone." His voice was a whisper.

Vikki nodded. "Dr. Brandon?"

"Yes." There was a pause. "Were you in the morgue earlier?"

Vikki was thrown off. "Was I at the morgue earlier?" she repeated, trying to buy herself time to think. Nothing came to mind. "Yes...we'll talk about that later. What does the result say?"

Dr. Brandon cleared his throat. "Two things stood out. She had a high creatine kinase, CK, as we already suspected from the taser. We also found barbiturates in her system." His voice was all business.

Vikki knew that barbiturates were used as sleeping pills not too long ago before benzodiazepines became more favored. High doses produce deep unconsciousness and can be used as general anesthetics.

"Barbiturates, when used during psychiatric examinations,

reduce voluntary inhibition," Dr. Brandon said. "And I think that's what the perp used it for."

"Can you elaborate?"

The ME blew out a breath. "The patient on barbs, when asked a question, would answer truthfully. Sometimes it's called truth serum."

"Isn't that hogwash?"

"The results are not consistent," Dr. Brandon said. "But there's no doubt it lowers voluntary inhibition. Security organizations won't own up, but there's a general belief that it's still used in clandestine interrogations. The victim was probably subdued with the taser, then injected with barbiturates to obtain the combination to her safe."

"Who could have access to it?" Vikki already knew the answer.

"Pharmacists, pharmacy technicians, doctors, nurses—hospital staff that handle medication," said Brandon.

A chill traveled down Vikki's spine. Sally Bolton was Jessica's friend and also a nurse. She fits the profile. "Thanks. I'll talk to you later."

"You better, bye."

Gomez returned. He dangled an iPhone in a plastic bag in front of Vikki.

She told him what Dr. Brandon had said. "I think Sally was at the estate sale with Jessica. She heard them talk about keeping lots of cash handy." Vikki pursed her lips, shaking her head. "I don't think Penne was the man on the video."

Gomez handed the plastic bag with the iPhone to Vikki. "Have Penne show you the photo. I'll see what information I can get about Sally Bolton. I'll also check with Santiago about their alibi with Olive Garden."

Vikki entered the interview room and gave the phone back to Penne. He turned it on, tapped, and swiped. "There she is!"

Vikki gazed into the calm, pale face of Sally Bolton. A strand of red hair crossed her face. She stood between a smiling Jessica Reid and Anna Ford. Vikki looked at Penne. "Who did Jessica say she was?"

"Her friend," Penne said. "I think their sons are in the same class in school or something like that."

Vikki stared at the picture, wondering what could've made Sally murder her friend. Desperation? Opportunity? She also had an accomplice. Who?

The interview door opened. Gomez stuck his head in. "Mattsen, you have to see this." He waved some documents in the air.

"Excuse me." Vikki stepped out and shut the door.

Gomez inhaled and said, "Sally Bolton, thirty, nurse. Never been arrested. Has a lot of debt—student loans, car loans, and credit cards maxed out. Collectors are calling. There's no breathing room.".

Vikki did a one-shoulder shrug. "That's a normal debt portfolio for many people."

"That's motive," Gomez said. "A few thousand dollars in her bank account would make her breathe easier—open her airway."

Vikki shrugged. "Maybe. What else do you have?"

"She's married to this piece of work, William Bolton. He has a rap sheet as long as the Appalachian Trail. Assault with a deadly weapon, theft, drunk driving, domestic violence. He'd used her as a punching bag on several occasions. A few times, she'd called nine-one-one but refused to press charges. He just finished a one-year sentence for growing marijuana. Like, walked away a free man a week ago."

Vikki let out a sharp breath. "Any jail time is like attending graduate school with emeritus professors as your instructors. Maybe he learned a few things he needed money to put into practice." She glanced up. "Maybe it was him who talked her into committing a crime."

Gomez cocked his head. "Maybe Sally mentioned to her hubby that a pile of cash is sitting in Jessica's safe for the taking. And he says, let's go for it."

"Let's bring them both in and find out what they know. They might be in cahoots."

"The wife scopes them out, and the husband nails them," Gomez said.

Vikki tapped her lips with her forefinger. "Let's send uniforms to pick her up from the hospital. We'll go to the house and get the husband."

CHAPTER TWENTY-SEVEN

Vikki headed for the squad room exit just as McClane was coming in.

McClane stopped and stood Akimbo. "Detective Mattsen! The interview rooms are not an extension of your home. You interview the suspect, then move them along. It's not a holding cell while you figure out their guilt or innocence at your leisure."

Vikki was tired and didn't have time for McClane. She muttered an apology and walked on. The man was too tired to speak.

He was right. She'd forgotten Anna Ford was still in two. But apologizing would be capitulation. She was not ready yet. They would sort it out when they got back. Or whoever needed the room should put her in another place.

Vikki signed out a car. She rode with Gomez to Sally Bolton's apartment on Waldwick Street, a twenty-minute drive away. They rode in companionable silence.

Vikki's phone rang as she pulled into the parking lot of Sally's home.

"Mattsen."

"Hi, Victoria, this is Russo."

"Hey, Russo. How are you?" Officer Russo was the only one who called her Victoria. He'd said that was his mother's name, too. He also covered the department's underwater recovery unit. They'd worked together on a case on St. Ives Lake.

"We were close to St. Martin's hospital and responded to the call from dispatch. Sally Bolton didn't come to work today. Should we check her house?"

"Negative. Gomez and I just got to her apartment. Thanks for the offer."

"Happy to help," Russo said.

The building super, a thirty-something-year-old man, left whatever he watched on his phone to attend to them.

"We're here to see Sally Bolton in two-zero-six. Do you know if she's in?"

He said the family was in, but he'd gone to the bathroom at some point. "If their car is there, then someone is home." He pointed at the elevator.

Vikki knew someone was home because she'd parked behind the white Jeep Compass she recognized from her first night at the crime scene. So close they were touching, and she'd engaged her emergency break.

Gomez and Vikki rode the creaky elevator to the second floor.

Vikki knocked at apartment two hundred and six. "Sally Bolton. SIPD! Open up!"

They waited. No sound came from inside the apartment.

Someone must be home. Sally's car was in the parking lot. The hospital had said she was home. Vikki's stomach muscles tightened. Her pulse beat faster.

She knocked again, this time with the butt of her Glock. The sound echoed down the length of the empty hallway. "This is the police. Open the door!"

More silence.

Vikki knew they had to enter the apartment, even if she had to make up something. She narrowed her eyes, cocked her head, and cupped her ear. "Did you hear that?"

"Hear what?"

"I think it was a little boy crying for help. Kick the door down, Gomez. Hurry!" Vikki stepped aside.

Gomez's eyes widened. Then he nodded, the hint of a grin on his lips. "It might need more than one." He stepped back and gave the door a solid kick above the handle. The thin door flew open.

Vikki went in first. Gomez followed.

Vikki crouched low, the pounding in her heart in sync with the rushing sound in her ears. "SIPD! We are armed. Come out with your hands in the air!"

Vikki scanned the room. It was an open-plan layout. She took in the leather couch and a flat-screen TV on the wall—a coffee table with two controls and a game console.

Gomez, his gun in front of him in a double-handed grip, went to the right toward some doors, probably the bedrooms and bathrooms.

Vikki crossed the kitchen. Ahead of her was a bifold louver door. She pulled the handle. It folded back to show the washing machine and dryer.

"Clear," Gomez said.

Vikki said, "Clear." She headed for the door down a short hallway.

She grabbed the old-fashioned doorknob and twisted. It rattled in her hand. She opened the door and gave it a shove. It swung slowly to the side.

Vikki scanned the room—a rumpled bed with blue scrubs laid out on it. Shoes and clothes are scattered on the floor. She turned left and froze. A chair was jammed under the doorknob of what Vikki believed was the bathroom. "Gomez, here!" Vikki rushed to the door. "Anyone in there?" A whimper came from behind the door. Vikki removed the chair.

Gomez stood to her right, his gun ready. He nodded.

Vikki turned the knob and pushed the door open.

The odor hit her. It smelled like the monkey bars in their local park when she'd pressed her nose against them as a child.

The door stopped moving—it had hit something. But it was wide enough for Vikki to slip in. In only a black bra and panties, Sally Bolton lay in a pool of blood on the floor.

CHAPTER TWENTY-EIGHT

Vikki reached for Sally's writs. She felt something, then realized it was her own pulse, full and rapid. She removed her hand—flexed and released—then tried again. Then she felt it ."Call for an ambulance!"

Gomez holstered his weapon and unclipped his radio.

Vikki assessed Sally's situation. She had several cuts on her lips, which both looked like sausages. Her eyes were swollen and turning into slits every second that passed. The blood seemed to be coming from a head injury. She hoped it was just a scalp wound.

Sally's lips moved.

Vikki bent low. "Sally, this is Detective Mattsen. You're safe now. Who did this to you?"

"Stop him. He's got, my son." Her voice was weak. Words slurred from her busted and p lips. "He took Tony...he killed Jessica."

Vikki wanted to be sure. "Who?"

"William...I thought it was him coming back to finish me off. Someone called from work and said the police were coming to the house and looking for me. He-he murdered my friend and took my son."

In the background, Gomez spoke to dispatch, requesting an ambulance and backup. Good man.

Vikki remembered hearing the fire exit door slam shut when they'd got off the elevator. Sally's husband had a head start, but she had to try.

Vikki adjusted Sally's leg and opened the door wider. Gomez stepped in.

"Sally, remember Detective Mike Gomez?" Vikki asked.

She nodded.

"He'll stay with you. Help is on the way. I'm going to get your son back."

Vikki dashed out of the apartment like a bat out of a cave at dusk. Her footsteps thundered in the hallway as she ran for the fire exit. At the door, Vikki stopped. Was he waiting on the other side? She hesitated for a second. He was escaping, not laying an ambush.

She yanked the door open, expecting to be ambushed. Nothing happened. She took the stairs two at a time, touching the handrail now and then for support. Any misstep would result in a broken ankle.

The stairs opened into the lobby. Vikki sucked in the air.

The receptionist saw her. His eyes widened. "He...he went that way." He pointed at the exit.

Vikki burst through the door into the afternoon sun. She blinked rapidly, adjusting from the dark stairwell to the bright sunlight.

The wail of police sirens got closer. Good.

Vikki pulled her gun. She knew precisely where Sally's husband was going. She crouched low and headed for the unmarked Explorer she'd signed out.

The Compass slid from side to side, hemmed in on all four sides by parked cars, its engine screaming bloody murder. White smoke and the smell of burning rubber filled the air. William Bolton was in the driver's seat, trying to push the Explorer out of the way with the Compass.

The sound of the police siren was loud. A cruiser came to a screeching stop in front of the apartment building. Vikki breathed a sigh of relief when Officer Russo and another officer rushed out of the police cruiser.

Vikki waved.

Russo squinted. "Victoria?"

Vikki hadn't seen Sally's son yet, but he must be with his father. She pointed. "Suspect is in the white Compass! He has a hostage. Assume he's armed!"

The driver's-side door of the Compass burst open. Sally's husband must have realized he wasn't going anywhere in the car.

William Bolton, glad in a sweat-soaked white wife beater and blue jeans, got out of the car. He beckoned to someone inside the vehicle. The person's head barely came up to the dash—Tony. Vikki took a step closer.

William Bolton glanced around. His eyes were wild and red.

Vikki pointed her Glock at his center mass. "Put your hands in the air! You are surrounded!"

William Bolton's mouth fell open. He spotted Russo closing in from his left. Maybe he hadn't expected the fast response.

"Don't do anything stupid!" Vikki said. She took another step closer. Her gun was held in a two-hand grip.

William Bolton's eyes darted from Vikki to Russo. He reached a decision.

His hand came up—pointed at Vikki.

"Gun! Gun!" Vikki's finger tightened on the trigger. It didn't need to end like this.

Three shots, three hits. William Bolton went down.

Vikki's pulse raced.

She approached cautiously. Bloodstains expanded on William Bolton's chest.

She kicked the gun away from his reach. It wasn't necessary. His eyes stared into the afternoon sky, unblinking. What was worse? Shooting William Bolton or killing him in front of his son?

Crushing pressure in her throat and chest reminded Vikki to breathe. She inhaled—the release of tension in her body welcomed.

CHAPTER TWENTY-NINE

The next day, Wednesday, Vikki sat opposite Captain Levin in his office. He looked immaculate in his navy-blue suit, white shirt, and red tie. He was pleased that the murder was solved and the perp had been taken out of commission.

"What about the couple? Have they left town?"

Vikki shook her head. "No. They'll stick around for Jessica's burial on Friday. Finding them gave us the break we needed."

"You did an exceptional job. Only ten years ago, I convinced you to enter the academy—look at you now."

"It was a team effort, sir," Vikki said.

Levin leaned forward. "I'll be speaking to the mayor soon. Can you tell me again how it all went down? The salient points."

Vikki exhaled and nodded. "Doug Penne and Anna Ford, the newly married couple, met up with Jessica Reid at an estate sale in Saddle River. They offered to buy the piece from Jessica and mentioned the power of cold cash in closing deals. Jessica mentioned she had a safe in her house."

Levin raised an eyebrow. "And the nurse...Sally was there with Jessica when this discussion took place?"

Vikki nodded. "Yes, and when she got home engaging in small talk with her husband over dinner, she mentioned it."

Captain Levin sighed. "That's like flashing a red scarf at a bull."

Vikki nodded. "As a criminal who'd just been released from jail, he saw how it could benefit him."

"It was premeditated," Levin said.

"All the way, sir. He ordered barbiturates online and borrowed his wife's taser without her knowledge. On Sunday, while Jessica's son was on a playdate with his son Tony, he took the car, went to her home, murdered her, and stole her money. He returned home and played video games with the boy whose mother he'd just killed.

"My God, that's cold-blooded," Levin said. "The worse of the worst."

Nodding, Vikki said, "Sally went to drop Jessica's son home after the playdate. And he found his mother's body."

The captain raised a finger. "So the GPS in the Compass confirmed the car was there when the ME believed the murder happened, and CCTV footage from a neighbor caught William Bolton when he went to the house?"

"Yes to both,' Vikki said."

Levin reached for the phone on his desk. "Keep up the good work. I have to call the mayor."

Vikki took the cue as a dismissal and left. Halfway to her desk, she froze. Dr. Brandon sat on her chair in scrubs showing off his cut physique. Heat rushed to her cheeks. She glanced around. Nobody was looking her way, but she knew the other detectives had eyes behind their heads.

She took a deep breath and approached. "Hey, what are you doing here?"

"I came for the explanation on why you pulled out one of my patients resting peacefully in her cabinet."

Vikki knew the truth would always set you free. "Oh, about that—we needed access to a biometrically protected phone during our investigation. The morgue is downstairs, the patient was there, and all we needed was a finger."

"Is that right," Dr. Brandon said. "Are you familiar with the Fourth Amendment to the US Constitution?"

Vikki rolled her eyes. "I am. But I understand those rights end when the individual's life ends."

Dr. Brandon nodded. "True, but by accessing the contents of her phone without a warrant, you trampled on the rights of others."

Heat flushed through Vikki. Why was everyone so concerned about covering their butts?

The ME continued. "There are proper ways to do things."

Vikki's nostrils flared. "Look, it was an emergency. A mother and her son are alive because of that intervention."

Dr. Brandon's nostril flared.

Vikki knew the conversation wasn't going as he'd antici-pated from his facial expression.

He glanced at his watch. "What if we continued this conversation over dinner?"

Vikki wanted to say yes, but he'd riled her up. "Let me think about it."

He rose from her chair. "You know where to find me."

CHAPTER THIRTY

Vikki, Angie, and Susie sat in Flame and Frost on the shore of Lake Mohawk. They were making up for the last get-together, which ended when Vikki was called off to investigate a homicide.

"You better turn your phone off this time," said Angie. "We must see this to the end. Having to make up again will be a little too much."

Vikki took a sip from her Hennessy and Coke. "I think it's a good idea." She brought out her phone and turned it off. She made a mental note to remember to turn it back on when she left.

Susie took a swig from her Corona bottle. "So, Vikki, how do you feel?"

Vikki cocked her head. That was an awkward question. "How do I feel about what?"

"You know." Susie raised a shoulder. "Taking a life. I've only seen people shot on TV."

Angie glared at Susie. "Susie, it's like asking a soldier if they've ever killed someone. It's their job, and in the realm of one of those questions, you don't ask. What do you expect her to say? She feels great!"

I'm looking forward to doing it again!"

Vikki tapped her lip with a finger. It was a thought-provoking question. It was kill or be killed. She'd chosen to live. At the academy, she and other cadets had spent time at the range, learning how to shoot. She'd spent extra time perfecting her shots. As Angie had said to her, it was another day at the office. Maybe later in life, it might become an issue. She decided to change the subject.

"So, Susie, any news from Rhode Island?"

Susie shook her head slowly, looking like the kid who'd eaten the missing cookie.

Definitely hiding something, thought Vikki.

"I don't know yet, but maybe I might get a visit."

Angie clapped. "Keep us posted." She sipped her drink and said, "Now, Vikki, back to you again. What are you doing? Or not doing with Dr. Brandon?"

Vikki's nose flared as she remembered her last encounter with him. A tingling swept up the back of her neck and across her face. She was so embarrassed. "I'm not doing anything with him. And I don't plan to do anything with him, period."

"Ouch," Susie said. "Am I missing something here? I don't know who this Dr. Brandon is, but you seem defensive." She lowered her head and glanced from Angie to Vikki. "That was a bit forceful. Are you trying to convince us or convince yourself?"

Vikki raised her hands and dropped them. "Are you a psychologist? You ask such probing questions."

Angie winked. "That's Susie for you. She gets right to the point." She took another sip from her glass. "Girlfriend, all I'm saying is this. This guy loves you. He's tackling his wanderlust personality, all because of you. A knight in shining armor doesn't get better than this."

Susie's eyebrows narrowed. "What? Come on, Angie. There's always something better out there."

Angie giggled. "Of course, but you have to find it. And when you find it, maybe you're not what it's searching for."

For a moment, the women fell silent. The sound of nearby conversations, the gurgling of the lake, and the croaking of frogs filled the void.

Goosebumps appeared all over Vikki. Angie had just dropped a golden nugget.

Maybe Vikki was too hard on herself.

"It's like that comet that shows up every seventy-six years." Angie snapped her fingers repeatedly. "What's its name again?"

"Halley's Comet," Susie said.

"Yes! By the time Halley comes around again, everything has changed." She pointed at Vikki. "Get on that Bronco now and make it yours while he's still interested in you."

The End.

Prologue

Beauty queens seemed to fade into oblivion—it never crossed Paige Arden's mind that missing queens turned into dead girls. You couldn't become Miss America without participating in the process. Nor win the Power Ball jackpot without buying a ticket—Paige Arden wanted it all.

First, she needed a portfolio from a well-known photographer. She'd heard about small-town beauty queens hitting it big. Going to New York for a photo shoot had opened her eyes to the possibilities. It could be her.

At the studio, she saw girls living the life she imagined for herself down the road. They wore the best fashion designer outfits, Rolex watches, expensive jewelry, and rich boyfriends at their beck and call. The smell of success was in the air, and Paige inhaled much of it.

She could win Miss Sussex County, Miss New Jersey, then the coveted prize of all, Miss America.

"But you have to go for it," Mark said while he snapped away with his Nikon. The mechanical double-shutter sound of the camera filled the air. "Pout your lips for me, honey."

The camera made the now familiar whining sound.

"Beautiful! You are a natural."

Snap. Snap.

"Make a face like you just tasted the best cheeseburger ever." Mark laughed. "I know you don't eat fast food."

The camera whined.

"Yes!"

That was Saturday.

Sunday evening, Paige scanned her room in her small apartment and thought of the future.

As the reigning queen of St. Ives Beauty & Brains Pageant, she'd already seen firsthand the attention it brought. Men who were way above her pay grade suddenly noticed her. She'd showed up like a shooting star.

And most of all, they all wanted her. For the first time in her life, she could choose what she wanted and not be forced by circumstance.

She stood in front of her closet, took a deep breath, and blew it out. "Paige, what would it be?"

Her iPhone rang. She removed the blanket and reached

for it on her nightstand. It was her mother, and she'd called a few times. Paige unplugged it from the charger.

"Hi, Mom."

"Paige! About time. I've been trying to get hold of you. How was New York?"

"Great but exhausting. I've been sleeping all day. I didn't know photo shoots were this demanding!"

"Well, that's life," her mother said. "Contrary to what people say, the best things in life are not free. You have to work for them. I'm glad you had fun. You took plenty of pictures?"

"Oh my God—a lot. Mark said I have the looks to go far in the industry. It was all up to me."

Her mother paused. "And Mark is...?"

"The photographer. But it would take a lot of commitment, especially since I love my day job at the school, too."

"I was going to ask you about that," her mom said. "Well, you have time to think about it. We'll talk some more when you come over."

A glance at the wall clock told Paige she'd better get out of bed, shower, and get ready for her date.

Paige was in and out of the bathroom. She'd shampooed her hair and dried it. The shower was a good place to think. Now she had a better idea of what to do between her day job and becoming a super beauty queen.

Tonight she'd wear something simple. It was only dinner. A pair of distressed jeans and a black blouse. Cat-eye makeup and a light skin-tone foundation.

She slipped on her underthings and her clothes. Paige hadn't worn her cowboy boots in a while. She wore a pair of cotton socks and was about to put on her boot when there was a knock on her door.

Paige checked the time. She wasn't late yet. She walked to the door and looked through the peephole. Her lips parted in a smile. She removed the security chain, unlocked and opened the door.

She cocked her head and smiled. "Hey, you. Come in." Paige turned and headed for her room. Behind her, the door clicked shut, and the lock turned. She reached for her cowboy boots.

"This is CNN." The sound came from the TV.

Paige giggled. "Make yourself at home while I get into these boots. I have some juice in the fridge if you're interested."

She sat on her bed, her back to the door, and bent down to pull up the boot while she forced her foot down. One foot was in. Paige was working on getting the second boot in when she felt a presence behind her.

She glanced over her shoulder. "You came to help? I'm almost done. One leg to go."

Paige's blouse tail must have ridden up because she felt a cold, clammy hand on her waist.

She whirled. "What are you—?"

The fist caught her on the jaw—propelled her forward. Pain exploded in her head. She fell, landing on her side.

Paige got on her hands and knees. She tasted blood. "Oh my God... Why?" She sounded funny. Blood dripped from her mouth like the first raindrops before a downpour.

The kicks came in a relentless torrent. Her face, stomach, thighs, head— all were pummeled. A veil of darkness shrouded her before the world faded away.

Chapter 1

Homicide Detective Victoria Mattsen, Vikki for short, stood in line at the coffee shop. The smell of java, freshly baked croissants, bacon, and eggs forced saliva into her mouth. She swallowed, hoping the line would move faster.

Three people were in front of her. The cashier repeated the order of the person she was attending to. "Medium French vanilla coffee, black. Egg and cheese on a buttered English muffin. Do you want it toasted? That will be..."

Vikki tuned out. She was dressed in a black pantsuit and black blouse. She subconsciously tugged down at her suit to make sure it hid her holstered Glock 19. She wondered what this week would be like at work.

She'd come a long way from her early twenties when she'd joined the police force. The murder of her friend, Alexis, and her dad, Mike Devoe, made her decide to join the police. On her first week as a rookie, an encounter with some criminals changed her life. She'd done things she ordinarily wouldn't have done for the next ten years.

"I didn't know I was going to meet you here," said a familiar voice behind her.

She knew that voice. A tingle ran down her spine. Vikki smiled...[click here for next in series]

ABOUT THE AUTHOR

Ifeanyi Esimai is a mystery and crime writer and enjoys reading across different genres. When he's not writing or reading, he's exploring documentaries on museums and ancient history.

Click here or the image to get all ten books!

Get a FREE copy of The Rookie!

Join my reader group for updates, giveaways, teasers, and a FREE copy of the prequel - The Rookie. Click here or scan the QR code